Off Island

a novel

Also by Lara Tupper:

A Thousand and One Nights (a novel)

Off Island

a novel

LARA TUPPER

Encircle Publications, LLC
Farmington, Maine U.S.A.

Paperback ISBN 13: 978-1-948338-82-0
E-book ISBN 13:978-1-948338-83-7
Kindle ISBN 13: 978-1-948338-84-4

This is a work of fiction. All characters and events portrayed in this novel are either products of the author's imagination or used fictitiously.

Editor: Cynthia Brackett-Vincent
Book design: Eddie Vincent
Cover design: Deirdre Wait
Cover images © Getty Images

Published by: Encircle Publications, LLC
PO Box 187
Farmington, ME 04938
Visit: http://encirclepub.com
Sign up for Encircle Publications newsletter and specials
http://eepurl.com/cs8taP
Printed in U.S.A.

For my mother,
Jill Kaplan Tupper,
who helped me see off island,

and in memory of my grandmothers,
Audrey Mendelsohn Reben and
Elizabeth Fowle Tupper,
who showed me many colors.

Off Island

PART ONE

(Where Do We Come From?)

PART TWO

(What Are We?)

PART THREE

(Where Are We Going?)

Part One

Pure color! Everything must be sacrificed to it.
—Paul Gauguin

You can't get there from here.
—Anonymous (someone from Maine)

The Painter

New England, 1903

1

THE NORTHERN ISLAND LOOKED best in morning light: slices of sheer cold rays on rugged pines and cliffs, the gray-blue sea below. The edges were glacier-pocked and the painter could imagine the ice sheets creeping over and creeping back, dumping bits of land where no land had been before. Mornings, the rocks looked like glaciers still, locked and frozen in mid-tumble toward the sea.

If you squint you can see clear to Portugal, the island Pastor had told him.

This reminded him.

Decades ago, on a ship to Peru, the painter's father had said, "Look hard and you'll see your hairy aunt waving from the dock in Lima." Bile had filled the boy's throat, his body lodged in the bow as the ship pitched like a small tree in the strong storm. His father had wanted him to focus on a far-away place. He lifted his son with solid arms again and again as he spit up over the side.

But when the ship reached Peru, no one waited at the dock, not even a priest. Lima was miles from the shore, the boy soon discovered. And his father wasn't there to point out which hairy aunt.

His father's heart had stopped mid-journey. *Bad heart*, he'd heard the Captain say.

It was one part of a dim, implanted memory: four years in Peru with his sad, distant mother, the particulars repeated by his mother's relatives so often the boy inherited the memories too. Not just the keeling of the ship and his queasiness, but the funeral at sea, the bulk of his father wrapped and sheeted and cast swiftly from the deck.

Now, from the island in Maine, the painter tried but failed to see Portugal.

He couldn't see Denmark either, where his own sons waited.

Not that his vision wasn't excellent. His eyes and mouth seemed braced for something unpleasant, his brow dented with squint-lines. At the glass in his rented room he prodded at the lines, his hawkish nose weathered by sun. And absinthe, perhaps. His beard was still a tawny reddish color, a hearty shade of rust. *Good-looking bugger*, he'd thought that morning. *Robinson bloody Crusoe.*

Now, on the cliff, the painter stooped, hearing a sharp rustle behind him on the trail—*Pastor? Landlady?*—the shush of thick clothing. He listened for voices, then twisted himself up to see two day-trippers in long, white dresses.

He plunked down foolishly in the raspberry bush again and waited.

"Look," said one. "A painter at work!" Then they walked on, laughing like gulls, pointing at distant Port Clyde.

The painter smelled the fruit about to turn, felt the tug of thorns on his pant leg. He plucked a pink berry and was disappointed to taste more seed than juice. He stayed there, squatting in the bush, until the laughter was gone.

The painter hadn't been off island yet, not since his arrival. What would be the point? He wasn't a promiscuous man in that regard. The light had become progressively more concentrated, less watery as the summer weeks passed. And now the cliffs required his full attention.

The islanders were tricky too, with their hard expressions, their slow way of speaking or not speaking—such a loudness in what wasn't said. The men were sturdy and barrel-chested, ready to shoulder lobster traps and strings of buoys heavy with seawater. The women had legs that could plant themselves into the ground and bear weight. They hauled things—laundry and children, herring for salting, ice for cooling, drums and casks of things shipped from away and dumped at the pier. There was churning and sound in daylight, all the warm hours utilized as the painter hid on the trails, his heart impious, his hands not put to proper use.

He tried to avoid the other painters too, dozens of them from Europe and worse, all peering out to sea in odd hats. They chose the paths closest to town (less lugging) and so he chose the path closest to the cliffs.

It was his dealer's fault—he'd lodged the notion long ago. *Go north! An island to yourself again, mon ami. Not like Polynesia. Get the paintings done quickly. Get them back fast for me to sell.*

He was a greedy bastard. A good dealer, a better friend. But dead wrong about the island being empty. *He was fucking Mette, probably. Or Mette was fucking him.*

He waited for a swoop of anger or jealousy at the thought.

But it was their arrangement. It was why she'd sent him away, wasn't it? To get him far from her house and the things he might wreck. Their children, for instance. Their savings.

No—this island wasn't at all like the warmer places with brown girls and their well-kept huts. The pole for his absinthe to cool in the well. The *hybride* would be two? Yes, two. Little Aline. Another Aline, now that the first was gone.

But of course not another.

He'd changed his mind on the docks at Le Havre, thinking of his wife and her orders, remembering what his dealer had suggested. He'd gone ahead and changed his booking, endured the stink of steerage. Saw the nub of land as the famous Captain Smith might have: a flat cake of earth buffering more—two islands, really. One protecting the other with a harbor in between, just wide enough for a ship to pull through. The blind luck of geography! An island saved from hard seas on one whole side, the side where the fishing could be staged, the part where the houses could crop up. Fish houses for bait and buoys and traps and lines. Little gray sheds weathered with boards for walkways, built on stilts to keep the water away.

The rest was all cliffs and woods with wild deer. And painters much too tame for his tastes.

He pulled himself up from the brambles, knees cracking, once the skirts were long gone. He moved his easel farther from the path and closer to the cliff edge, waited for the mainland to disappear, for his dead daughter and living wife to leave him, until the wind and cliffs and sea were all he knew.

2

THE PASTOR CALLED HIMSELF *Canuck* and talked with his pale, fine-boned hands, just as the painter did. He stored a barrel of sweet, grassy beer in his basement and hidden bottles of absinthe on high shelves. They'd spent most nights together in this way, drinking in the Pastor's small, oaken den.

Until the Pastor offered the use of his tub, there were blemishes on the painter's cheeks and a scent in his clothes difficult to ignore, a kind of saline crotch rot he'd smelled on *les putains* in Montmarte. There was a blistery sore down there sometimes too, something he didn't care to think about, something that reappeared and oozed occasionally.

It was difficult for the painter to bathe in his own rented room. The tub was placed just under the steepest part of the roof and his back wasn't always up to it. After hours at his easel he felt a thick and angry welt ripping along his torso. But at the Pastor's he was freshly scrubbed, drying by the fire, a borrowed robe flung over his lap. The Pastor kept his eyes averted and offered the Parisian more ale.

The painter asked about the names of island things and kept a list in a small, red notebook: the cliffs he stood on, the humps of land in the distance. He wanted to see a map and the Pastor found one, brittle and torn at the edges, mugs weighing the corners down. Slowly, he began to see where he was.

The trails, said the Pastor, had been pounded by human feet for close to three centuries, more if you counted the Indians, whom nobody did, bludgeoned by Captain Smith and company long ago.

Such an odd accent, thought the painter. The Pastor stretched out his a's like the locals and his r's sometimes disappeared completely. To walk a great distance was to walk quite *fah*.

"Tell me," the Pastor said, leaning to fill his guest's cup again, the fire licking around them. "You are a savage too?"

It was hard to know what the Pastor meant by this exactly. The painter felt his eyelids droop from the smoke, the beer. The fire made sharp, excitable shadows on the walls. The room itself felt like a burning thing.

"Abenaki, Penobscot, Wawenock. Brilliant names, yes?" The Pastor continued. "*Ah-beh-nack-ee.*"

"My mother was Peruvian," the painter offered. "And I do enjoy the sun, Father." Father? That probably wasn't correct.

The Pastor watched a spark land near the painter's stocking foot. "But you're French," he said at last. "No would ever suspect." He cleared his throat—a sign of polite dismissal—and waited for the painter to dress himself. "The sun, the sea," he said, as the painter let the borrowed robe fall to the ash-dusted floor. "They say the light is good—so much water and air. The light bends in an unusual way because of this. Is it so? I am clearly not a painter."

The Frenchman stood between the Pastor and the fire. He bent to gather his shoes. "The light, yes," he offered. "Though I think it is the color you mean. The colors are *vivide*, no? I have seen something similar in Pont-Aven—I have gone there many times before. Very religious people leading a simple life. Like you, Father, except the women there have large...hats. You have seen this?"

Still shirtless, he sketched for the Pastor the hats and the tits of the pilgrim women in Pont-Aven, hats like birds, tits like melons.

"How unusual," said the Pastor, eyes darting at the small notebook with the black string, and the drunk, dark man before him with his boots untied.

"My friend Vincent was there," said the painter. "He also preferred I bathe in his presence."

The Pastor said nothing.

"You would have liked him, I think. Except he was pale, not dark." *And dead*, thought the painter, which was too bad. "I go to my landlady now."

"Yes," said the Pastor, clapping his hands. "How is Lizzie? Giving you fresh sheets, I trust? And doughnuts?"

The painter left without answering, a full, wet flask of absinthe bulging his pocket, which the Pastor pretended not to see.

3

THE PAINTER WOKE, AS he usually did, with a steady pain in his temples and a fierce need to urinate, with the sounds of Lizzie working hard below, shouting to her girl for something called *thahwhisk.* Then the beating of something in a bowl.

By separate entrance the painter could creep in and out when he liked, up steep stairs in need of paint. The landlady heard him, of course.

Lizzie. Now shouting at her girl for flour from the store. Busy woman—up early, home late. Mornings cooking, afternoons at the Fish House apparently gutting clams and lobsters for chowders and stews, sold to tourists. Weekends as a chambermaid at the Island Inn. She'd mentioned her island duties to the painter more than once.

He peed, then looked through the smudged window at the narrow portion of sand outside. The islanders called it Fish Beach, where men kept their traps and buoys, and hacked up the occasional tuna or dogfish, red oozing into the dull brown sand. Lizzie would have made a fine lobsterman, hauling crates in the wet and cold with her mannish gait and a face a little like his own—broad eyes, dark skin. (Something of the savage in her too? Wawenock?) She had a way of hunching around that wasn't at all ladylike, like she could crush a man. Maybe she'd crushed one or two before? Her husband was long gone—dead or missing, the painter wasn't sure which.

Something more specific gnawed at the painter in bed today—the savage question. Peru. Why had the Pastor asked him this? *But you are French*, he'd concluded.

It was hard to think clearly at that hour. *Allez*. He should get out and work. The light—catch the light. The Pastor was right about this, the island sucked in color in a most unusual way.

*

He said the names of the cliffs to himself as he walked the path, sun hot on his hands, coffee taste in his mouth: *Black Head, White Head, Pulpit Rock*. The English words were blocky. His lips were chapped and he sipped from his flask to wet them, one tiny slurp, the absinthe he'd taken from the Pastor. His easel was right where he'd left it, a bulky model, one he'd had to buy from McFadin's, the lone general store on island where everything was overpriced. At least for the artists—full nickels more.

With the Pastor's help he'd secured an account and the painter went in daily for bread, milk, paints or brushes. The surly boy behind the counter, the oldest son of the school mistress, ticked boxes in a bulky ledger.

"Brings it to three dollars," the boy said, the side of his mouth sneering up. It was how he was born, the painter could see, a shift of the chin and lip to one side. Still, it seemed directed at him. "Credit?"

"Yes, thank you," he'd told the boy in French.

His previous easel, a lovely, lightweight thing, had been handmade by the robust and handsome hotelier in Pont-Aven he'd come to know so well. It was cedar and had smelled lovely for weeks. Worn dull by the time he lost it, pocked with flecks of yellow and blue from the batch of pictures he'd left behind. That easel was ruined during the latest crossing: the casks of beer, the fiddlers playing late. His cabin smelled of vomit and sweat, like the many men before him unable to bathe for weeks. It was like his Navy days, when he still believed new places could alter him for good.

The tug of it, still—a vessel. The ease in pulling away, in watching a familiar place go. It was how absinthe—or afternoons in the hut with the girl—could make him feel sometimes.

But it didn't last. He had to keep moving or drinking or both. And the sex was always done too quickly.

Stop it and get to your easel, a Mette-like voice said. *This is why I sent you—to paint.*

But the old, good easel! Left behind in his locked steerage cabin, bound for the new island. He'd been on Main Deck, sketching. A stump of a pencil, a cheap pad with scratchy paper—not his best supplies, not his best work, but that hadn't been the point.

There were so many bored women with rich husbands, but only one lady in green, the shiny layers of her skirt alternately emerald and pine. Her face was fine-boned, her lips two thin lines, barely lips at all. It would be hard to make her mouth bend into his.

That had been it, most likely, not the shades of green but her very small lips. And her height. In shoes she was several inches taller than the painter. She was a slim, lipless giant to fell.

He'd wanted to see her bare shoulders and he told her so on the Promenade Deck. She laughed tightly and after two hours of small talk and a vial of absinthe in her afternoon tea, he managed to lure her to her own A Deck cabin, her husband distracted, "rapt" as the woman had said—a word the painter hadn't understood at first—having made it to the final round of the bridge tournament. After one more aperitif, she let him remove her blouse, her cheeks red, two small ovals high on her cheekbones. It was so easy to convince her take off more, and soon she was naked, skin papery white, the space between her small breasts wide and hollow. The painter placed his hand there and felt how warm she was, how her heart thumped heavily. He slid the hand along her belly without kissing her. Then he pushed into her roughly, unable to wait, grunting and farting—and yet it wasn't him at all. It was just a version of himself he watched from a great, dim distance.

Liar, he heard the Mette voice say.

He missed his wife. He did. Even as he fucked the Bostonian.

As soon as his privates shrunk back to normal, he began to compose another letter in his head, something about the momentum of each new *liaison*—how this should have reeled him farther and farther away from her like a stone flying fast down a cliff.

It wasn't until later, smoking alone at the stern, that he remembered (*Merde!*) the sketchbook. He smoked some more and waited until the sea and moonless sky became one continuous black wall. He returned to his cabin.

He saw that his lock had been cracked, felt that the stale air inside had shifted. He saw his belongings as a stranger would: battered leather satchel, bottles on the floor.

Under his sheets he found his easel, cracked into splintery pieces by the woman who'd woken groggily, scrambled for her clothes, and found the sketch of another woman—one much lovelier and twice as large. His wife, to be precise. He'd taken the time to label the sketch accordingly: *Mon épouse.*

For the rest of the crossing, the painter wore a hat with a broad woolen visor. The woman stayed on Promenade with her husband, peering over his shoulder at his cards. At night the painter watched them from just outside the ballroom. They waltzed in neat green and black, her cheeks bright with the same high flush.

Good, he'd thought. At least they were having relations again.

Before disembarking, the painter had salvaged his good paints from his broken easel (vermillion, teal). They'd lasted his first week on the island, and then he'd had to buy more from the surly boy at McFadin's. He'd wanted to write to Mette for paints, but he should probably mention to her first: He'd lied. Or neglected to let her know his change of plans. He wasn't in the South Pacific at all.

Best to wait on that. Soon he'd sell a painting to one of the day-trippers. He could go for proper supplies off island then.

He sipped from his flask. *The light. Don't waste it.* He considered the line of Port Clyde. He snapped a purple clover flower from a bush beside him and chewed. He'd meant to buy a pastry from the store, the same sad bun he'd seen there the day before.

At last he slid a mossy green line across the canvas horizon. He could just make out the mainland—a curve of land smudged and bleary, a flank turned over away from him. A hip swelling out of the sea.

4

THE SUN, ACCUSING HIM, set over the lesser island across the harbor, the painter's room now dark with pink edges. Someone pounded at the door.

Is there smoke? The painter hurried to answer, thinking in his blurry state that a fire had spread, that the deep oranges in the sky were reflections of the island blazing and that someone—the Pastor—had come to save him.

But it was Lizzie, just done with her Fish House shift, smelling of bait oil and sea, a stack of linen against her chest, folded severely. "Sheets," she said. "Come to do the linens."

"*Merci.*"

"Thought you'd be out. You busy?"

"A nap. *Petite.*" She was his height exactly. She didn't smile. She stayed to do them herself, smoothing the edges with large, chapped hands. He pretended not to watch her, busied himself with tea and spoons, but she left her cup steaming, nodded and left, the force of the door making the room rattle after she'd gone.

"Eye wood lick une towelle, please," the painter tried the next morning in the glass, his French-English dictionary propped on the faucet. Not, *Je voudrais une serviette de bain, s'il vous plait*, but, *I would like a towel, please.* The sound of it was odd, the consonants jumbled. It should have been easier to say because there were fewer syllables. But he wouldn't be able to preface it with "How was your day? Were the fish good to you? Did they mind being cut open by your pretty hands? I have had a most inspiring day myself, Madame Lizzie, on the high cliffs of your wonderful and curious island. I spotted one deer and two seals and one black, loud bird I did not know the English name of. It made a sound like, 'A cawwee!' I wonder if you would accompany me some morning to help me with this; I would very much like to name this bird.

"That said, I am sorry to keep you, I know you are a busy woman. But would it be possible to have one more small towel for my washbasin? Just one more *serviette de bain, si'l vous plait*? I am a very dirty man, you see."

This is how it had been with the quick-to-laugh Madame in Pont-Aven the summer she'd made him the easel. She was hearty and large. She'd taken to eating more pastries since her husband had become sick. She liked her sherry too, and the painter had treated her to several at the hotel pub, where she doubled as the barmaid.

One night he'd asked Madame for some accoutrement or other, a pillow or a bar of soap, when in fact he was fully stocked. Would she mind bringing it up herself? He slipped a bill under her sherry glass.

She'd understood what was meant by the request. She'd left the money. She hadn't been ashamed.

But this wasn't his intention with Lizzie, not yet. He needed a towel. He'd ruined the other one by using it to mop up his palette.

He met her on the beach as she trudged back from the Fish House.

"I can't understand you," Lizzie said. Her collar was damp and brown around the neck.

"Eye wood lick *une towelle*, please," he said again. "A tow-el."

"I gave you a towel."

"Another, *s'il vous plait*? It's just I would like to wash—"

"This ain't no ho-tel," she said. "You want another, you can rent another. One nickel. You bring me the money, I'll give you the towel." She angled a shoulder past him and carried her pot of clams into her kitchen, shutting the door behind.

He watched the door, thinking perhaps it was a joke. That she would peek out with a toothy smile to say, "Surprise!"

But the door stayed closed. He heard her daughter thumping around behind the curtain, asking if it was too late to go fishing for crabs.

A nickel! Ridiculous! He retreated to his room to consider the alternatives: a brown curtain, thick and faded? He wasn't certain he could re-tie it in the same way. The smudges from his hands and arms would stay there unless he washed those too. His own clothes were filthy, all of them. The small throw rug was coarse with sand from Fish Beach. The blankets on his bed he needed.

Fuck it, he thought, in French, and lit the flame beneath the kettle. He rubbed at the knots in his neck—from hunching over the easel, from stretching to see the bird behind the obtrusive pine. He needed a bath—but it seemed too early to see the Pastor.

He wished at that moment for Mette. It was Mette who'd bathed the children in the kitchen, oldest to youngest—the windows steamed, their mothers solid hands on them scrubbing. Aline, who'd liked to splash. With a full mug of ale he'd once tried to draw them bathing, the group he'd created.

Created? Corrupted, said his wife. *Now feed them, please.*

The painter gauged the slanted corner of the Lizzie's low ceiling, the raised tub; he poured in the steaming water. He waited. He couldn't wait anymore. His skin puckered gratefully.

By the time Lizzie walked in with the large white towel, the painter was rolling a cigarette (his second attempt, his fingers still damp). He'd manicured his left foot with a small knife he'd found in the drawer. He dripped, having decided to dry *au natural.*

Lizzie didn't draw back. She was used to flesh, had ripped it open for years at the Fish House. And she was growing accustomed to the odd ways of artists and foreigners on her island. She turned her head away, just the same. "Your towel, *Monsieur.*" She held it out to him at arm's length and he took it.

"*Mais je suis sans l'argent,*" he snapped. He rested the folded towel over his lap.

"You can get that nickel to me later," she said, backing out.

"No knocking?"

"I thought you were still in the bath," she said. "Thin walls. You haven't drained the water yet." This was true, a purplish well of it there still in the tub, the shade of Mette's hair on the easel that day. The dried streaks of it faint on his arms.

Lizzie allowed herself to look at him then, the beard, the swirls of black chest hair, the belly rounded like dough, his feet surprisingly small. She saw the paring knife on the counter, the metal file by his heel. He liked his toes neat. His fingers were such stubby wrecks, the paint forming dark trim underneath. His toes he could make better, at least.

Cleaned up he wasn't so bad, thought Lizzie. Not a handsome man, but an intense-looking fellow. Long nose, olive skin. Deep lines in his forehead from peering at things in the sun.

The painter recognized the gaze, one he'd used often: considering the body, assessing. He smiled at her then, letting his legs splay a little. "To look at the old guy, *n'est pas—*"

"Goodbye," she said, nodding as though she approved. "Keep warm."

He heard her quick steps on the stairs and then the whap of the front door. He lifted the towel and considered his pubic hair, the fine black hairs on his knuckles, the cave of the bellybutton. Remarkable what one could see post-bath, details in the sack of skin he lived inside. *Why cover it up?* His privates lifted a little at this thought. *Not bad for an old man.* He returned to his toes, goosebumps spreading. He giggled.

Below him Lizzie's own kettle boiled for tea.

5

"YOU SHOULD SLEEP MORE," said the Pastor from across the oaken table.

"There isn't time," said the painter, not meaning to flirt, but flirting: "The nights I save for you."

The Pastor cleared his throat. "It seems the island women have noticed you."

"They notice, I think, my rugged good looks."

The Pastor looked away from the painter's rugged good looks.

"They notice the artists. Anyone not smelling of lobster," the painter added.

"You'll come back again? Next summer, when the weather is good?"

"You want me to leave already?"

They paused. A tree branch scratched against the glass and made the Pastor turn.

"I'm a rude man, " said the painter. "I drink all the absinthe, and I have profane thoughts in the presence of a holy man."

The Pastor ignored this. "I mean, I should like to meet Madame Mette."

"I should like to meet her too."

The Pastor smiled. He was drunk, and he appreciated the Parisian's odd humor, odd French. "Lizzie's a hardworking one, no?

And her cousin? Have you met him yet?"

"The fish house man?"

"Vaughan. He likes to keep an eye on the tenants."

"*Tenant.* That's a very formal word for what I am," the painter said.

"I mean, be careful," said the Pastor. He gulped at his beer. "It's a small island; they'll find you. If they have a need to find you."

The painter leaned back in his chair and yawned. "You've tasted Lizzie's doughnuts? I haven't yet had the pleasure." He began to tell his favorite joke: the one about the baker.

"A French baker?" said the Pastor.

"Of course! He's Canuck, actually," said the painter. "And one day an ugly American man walks by the open window and catches the baker rolling the dough on his hairy chest, the dough meant for eating—for pastries and bread! The American is shocked. He's an ugly American but at least he's clean."

The Pastor shifted in his chair.

"The American watches and watches—the rolling back and forth—this is a very good French baker, he can see, very thorough about his dough. And then at last, when he can no longer contain his anger and disgust, the American storms into the kitchen and shouts at the baker: *'How can this be?'* The American is very tall, much taller than the poor, half-naked Canuck."

The Pastor's clasped his hands together, listening.

"The American says to the French man, *'You expect the people to eat this?'* And the baker says nothing, just looks at the American for a long time. He begins to peel the warm dough from his chest, his body dusted with flour, oily with sweat. The American helps him by pulling at pieces from his skin and throwing them angrily on the floor." The painter leaned forward. "Do you know what the baker finally said back to the American?"

The Pastor leaned back and let his hands fall to his lap.

"Do you know what the Canuck said to this American man in his kitchen?"

The Pastor cleared his throat. "*Je ne sais pas*. What? What?"

"The Canuck said 'If you think this I bad, you should see how I make the doughnuts.'"

The Pastor's knee banged against the table's underside.

"Do you get the joke?" asked the painter.

The Pastor swallowed and looked away.

"Do you want to see the joke?" the painter asked, quickly unbuttoning his fly. "You see? This is how he made the donuts."

The Pastor laughed, the expression on his face shifting from embarrassment to relief. Then he sensed, beyond the open shade, something else in the branches.

The painter heard it too (his empty glass rolling from the table, not breaking), the clink of a lantern against the pane. Boots on gravel turning away.

"*Allez*," the Pastor said, busying himself with the map, the jars.

"Yes, I go," said the painter, smiling. "*Voyez-vous demain*." He gathered his shoes.

"Yes, tomorrow," said the Pastor, as the door fell behind.

The painter left, but couldn't yet return to his room to hear the odd shifts of Lizzie lurking below, the waves spreading themselves back and forth—sad, slow sounds along the pebbled beach. There was joy in repetition, someone had said. *Whom?* For the painter the days were becoming very much the same: Wake with headache. Go to the shitty easel on the cliff. Stay for hours. Drink too much at the Pastor's. Take a bath or perhaps tell a dirty joke. But there was less joy, lately.

He walked back to the cliffs and his easel instead, tripping against the jumbled roots and rocks, the shapes of things sneaky in the dark. The moon wasn't bright, and he stared at it—*gibbous, like gibbons!* He could paint it this way, a shining monkey dimming out as the night sky around it, until the moon, overcome by too much blue, was just a white smudge no one noticed.

Mottled thoughts. *Idiot thoughts*, the Mette voice said.

"Fuck the cliffs!" he told her.

You're Icarus now? He saw the meanness curling around her lips. *You're bigger than all this? Your wife and children too*?

But you wanted me to go! Then he slipped with a jolt that made his head quite clear, felt the tough, old rocks digging in, felt the wetness on his palms. The rich, dead smell of fallen needles—how rusty they looked in daylight. He pawed around, lifted his hands to taste the saltiness.

Slumped on the path, blind and absurd in the dark. What if you died here, alone in the woods on an island?

He passed out, letting the earth cushion him completely.

6

STABBED BY COUSIN VAUGHAN, Lizzie thought at first. Or stabbed something himself—fed up with all the fish and caught himself a wild doe? But then she could see he'd only fallen, drunk in the night. She'd done the same herself once or twice before, flat-out on the Black Head trail. She could see he was in a state. Shat himself, smelled like. Gashes on his face and hands.

She'd come to chuck the lobster shells at Lobster Cove. (*Throw them back where they came from*, Vaughan had ordered.) Two buckets filled with broken tails and claws and insides, mosquitoes buzzing something fierce, the pull of the weight on her shoulders. She'd dumped the goop, the gulls squawking—*rats of the sea*. Then left the buckets on rocks. She wanted to climb to where the easel might be—see for herself what the tenant had mentioned. He said he left the paintings out there too sometimes for texture, for weathering.

He said a lot that sounded like crap. *Merde paresseuse*. Lazy shit just didn't want to lug his easel back and forth.

But on the way to find out for sure, there he was on the trail, the lump of him bloodied and still, the first light making it all a little holy-looking.

She hustled back to the boat shack then, got the wheelbarrow, pushed Prince Paris all the way back, with the gooped out lobster buckets perched on his stained, stinking lap. Then she hoisted him up the stairs.

He slept the whole day, then stumbled down from his room with a panicky look as the colors outside were pinky and blue.

"*Mon mains*," he said, and she looked at the swelling. Banged himself up good, a deep part near his thumb still open where a rock had stabbed in. She found the roll of Vaughan's fishnet, boiled it all, jabbed the needle in quick without warning. He hollered just like her girl.

"It'll hurt some," she said. "To paint." She filled the jelly jar to the rim with whiskey, and he drank it all. She got the bath going and pushed a clean towel in his arms, motioned for him to keep his hands out of the water. He nodded, and she saw he'd been crying from the shock—clean parts in the crow's feet around his eyes.

When he was bathed and calm again he kneeled in front of her, groping at her waist, smelling a little rank and fishy still, like sand and shells and the dirty, blue-gray sea.

"*Merci*," he said, weeping. "*Merci beaucoup*."

She pushed him away, but gently.

Later, alone, she felt for her own scars in the dark—where the fishhook went in, where the lobster claw clamped down, where the baby was cut out of her, just above the place where her dead husband had liked to breathe her in.

7

NEAR THE END OF JULY, Lizzie left two doughnuts for the painter at the bottom of the steps, wrapped in a towel to keep them warm.

The rest of the batch, the painter knew, would be sold at McFadin's for a nickel apiece. Because Lizzie had told him this, the painter wondered if he was supposed to pay for the donuts too.

He didn't. On Black Head, he measured the donut hole circumference with the Hairy Baker's frame of reference. *Not possible,* the painter decided sadly. He tossed the pastry from Black Head to see if a gull would snap it mid-throw. (It did.)

His thumb was raw, her stitches sloppy. *Who did she think she was?* He cringed at the memory, kneeling at her waist.

But the throbbing had stopped—he could work again.

The next Thursday Lizzie left two more and this time the painter decided to try a corner of the greasy thing, fatty and sweet, rolled in sugar, the color of chestnuts but yellow inside.

He dropped two nickels in her palm that night.

She was drinking from a mug in the seat of her landed dory, shoes off, pants rolled to cool her feet in the sand on either side. She was staring out at the harbor, the girl apparently asleep indoors.

"What for?" she said.

"The grease cakes," he said to tease her. "*Beignets.*"

"Doughnuts," she said. She pocketed the money.

"I know this," he said. "Doughnuts." It was a hazy night, the moisture in the air making everything sweaty. The gulls screeched further down the beach, beyond the breaker, feeding on fish-guts. He sat beside her in the rowboat without asking and wondered aloud about the buffer island across the harbor: the imposing, black hulk of it, the supposed Norse etchings on the windward side, the shell of the old hermit's house on the lee. A white-bearded man who'd sailed all the way from Ireland to get away. Lived with sheep and geese in a hut he built from driftwood and only rowed across the harbor to the big island when he needed food for himself and the animals. All of them long gone but the driftwood shack still there.

"All true," said Lizzie. Some days she didn't even see the other island, not really. A thing could disappear when you stared at it every day.

"I know," said the painter. "Not as beautiful. Boring." But to bump into an island by sea—to land there and stay awhile, as Captain John Smith had, as the *hermite* had. That would have been different. The land would have looked sacred, appearing just in time, just before they'd given up.

"I can help you with the baking, maybe," he said, and then he told her the doughnut joke. He liked the sound she made when she laughed, like his grandmother in Peru, pitching her neck back to let out the sound, like she was throwing something far.

"The holes, you make how?" he repeated. Lizzie barked out another peal that bounced to the hermit's house and back.

He wanted to push further, crack her open, keep her laughing. He could see it had been a while since someone had done this, shoved at her for fun.

"You know about my crazy house?" she said. "How it was lugged here from the mainland, already built?" She leaned back in the boat, folding an arm under her head.

She was silent for a long time before he realized she'd gone to sleep.

8

WHEN THE PAINTER CREPT out of his room and down the steps at his normal time, well past noon, Lizzie was gutting pogies in the Fish House.

He tipped his woolen cap. She saluted, knife in hand.

"Smells like a fine woman," he said.

"Smells like a man if you're from here."

Vaughan ducked in and emptied another bucket on the table. "Afternoon," he said without looking at either of them. Then he left.

"He talks too much I think," said the painter. He poked at Lizzie's shoulder.

"Doesn't have to talk," said Lizzie. "He owns half the island."

"He owns you also?"

She shooed him away with her knife.

On the cliff he thought of her compact body close in the rowboat and the fabric of his pants chafed at him. He leaned into the easel and rubbed himself against the base of it once, smearing his crotch with red. He rubbed himself again and then yanked his trousers down completely, crouching in the bushes, spilling onto his hand. He wiped his hand on a rock and hoped the gulls wouldn't come to investigate.

"You don't paint much," Lizzie said in the rowboat.

"Every day? This isn't enough for you?"

"I mean the paintings. I mean you haven't brought a single canvas back down from Blackhead."

"You are spying?" He had an urge to grab her then but didn't.

"You showing the gulls your work? A gallery up there?"

He wouldn't tell her where they were, but he'd sneaked them back, rolled them in a cardboard tube, stuck the tube down his pants, wondered if she'd noticed the bulge. They were worth something, this he knew. He'd hidden them behind the sofa and in an attic door he'd pried open with a knife. In the closet behind his naval pea coat, unworn since the crossing.

He wouldn't tell her this, but he did begin to tell her the truth about his work: He was so tired of the pretty light. It was just a lot of water and sun, sea and sky, the reflections causing tricks. What did the colors look like without all the refracting and reflecting? What was the color of the water *really*? He'd probably never find out.

And so the Blackhead cliff became a workplace, not a vista—just an apt place to be. The longer he stayed, the more he painted the things that weren't there: Fables, stories, pieces from Roman statues and island *tikis*. The stance of an Egyptian and the birth of Jesus and the shape of girl's naked body in bed, the dead daughter he couldn't bear to think of—he pieced together what seemed right at the time, with solid patches of outlined color. He told stories about the images that wouldn't go away.

He stopped then. He didn't explain all of it to Lizzie. Nothing about Tehura and her lovely Tahitian behind. He didn't tell Lizzie he'd started to take her stories too, that by day he sketched what she told him: the hermit, the Norse sailors, the crazy uncle who'd hauled his house across the bay. This is how he'd begin to know her better, by stealing her stories and making them his own.

At night he pictured her, one floor below. He imagined slipping a hand under her nightgown, curling his fingers into the warmth of her, feeling her chest push into him. Her body would bend and grind on its own, half-asleep. As the painter rubbed against the starched white sheets alone he was sure he heard something below, a sigh or a moan, slight and muffled.

It was possible—she'd seen him naked. She was only human.

"So what will be next? For your paintings?" she asked him in the rowboat.

"It's secret," he said to her. "I mean private. It's a very private thing."

9

THE PASTOR ONLY REVEALED the end of the house story: "Heaved it up the beach with a thick rope and a line of strong men." He had less patience for the painter, now that he spent his evenings with the landlady. It was lunchtime, and he didn't refill the painter's glass. "Vaughan was there—he pulled the rope himself. Ask him." He began to read the Melville book on the table, his face a sharp, lonely mask.

The painter did not ask Vaughan. He went to the post office after lunch, where he mailed his eighth letter to Mette. Not one in return. He tried not to worry about what this meant but the trying failed—the post office made his heart beat ragged. He expected Mette to appear behind the counter any day, ready with a knife.

"Turt Brewer the house-hauler was my uncle," said the postmistress. "Heard you've been asking."

"I know this," said the painter, who did not know this. He wanted to send the letter to his wife and be gone. "I hear already about the high tides, the patient man."

"High tides? Ice, more like. Bay froze over that winter and Turt humped the thing on blades all the way up the beach."

"Blades?"

"Ice skates. The blades that strap on shoes—strapped to the house instead. Hundreds of them. Had to get all of Bay Harbor to donate."

"*Un mensonge.* Made up story," said the painter.

"Ice skates for a house, that's the truth."

He pushed his letter toward her.

"What, you think I was around then?" She cackled, and it was Lizzie's laugh. She looked nothing like Lizzie. Red hair, complicated curls, a bust like a pigeon. She could balance a plate of doughnuts there if she wanted.

She counted out his change slowly. "I'm Elva," she said. "Lizzie's cousin." Her clean, neat fingertips were fine little shells. "And you're the new tenant from France." She slid the dull coins across the countertop and grinned at him.

"Elva's a liar and maybe the Pastor some too," said Lizzie. They were squished side by side in the boat again, leaning back. She smelled like turpentine from painting the Fish House.

"It was planned, an experiment. He wanted to test the currents and the capstan. He was clever that way." She stretched her neck around to look at the thing. "I wish he hadn't done, just the same." The lantern from her kitchen table made a narrow streak of light along the beach.

The painter didn't ask what a capstan was, but he could see her point. The cracked boards, the salt-sprayed windows. Drafty old cave, fish smells seeping up, oiling the insides. "No moon, *ce soir*," he said.

"None the night before neither," she said. Her lips were fleshy. She stuck her jelly jar in the sand and turned to him.

"*Reposez-vous*," she said.

"You speak French," said the painter, sitting up.

Then she slipped her hand down the waist of his trousers. Cool hands. He flinched, and pushed his own hand, still flaked with dried paint, under the fold of her skirt—*like bathing*, he thought, the comfort of skin when bones were chilled. The need for warmth, like bath water—even when the water was tepid. Her mouth was sour from wine.

"My girl is sleeping," she said. She squeezed his hand with hard little pulses and led him up the ramp, which creaked, to the boat shack. She shooed the cat from the open door. They stood for a moment, looking into the dim—there was no obvious place to lie down. The small windows were latched shut, dark with grime. The traps were stacked beside a loose pile of rope. The fish smell wasn't unpleasant—salty, not rotten. Something cured, preserved. She pulled the leather strap of his belt and caught the buckle before it clattered to the floor.

"There," she said and pushed him to a hidden pillow in the corner, greenish with mold. She undressed quickly and her hips were wider than his by two, he thought. "Thatta boy," she said. He grunted, and she shushed him. She slapped him on the back, then kissed him roughly, thrusting fast herself, until they seemed to be lifting the shack with their rocking.

"*Merde*," he said, letting his face fall into the musty pillow. The cat, who'd sneaked back in, mewed close to his ear.

It went on like this for the rest of the summer. Days painting, stony suppers with the Pastor, late nights in the boat shack with Lizzie.

10

MORNINGS, LIZZIE WAS SLOW at work, careful not to let the throb in her head move around.

Vaughan said, "Sleep well?"

"Like a princess," she said, stabbing at fish.

He let his eyes drift to Frenchman's room. Then he turned to shuck the pile of clams with his own sharp tool.

11

"GAY PAR-EE!" SAID ELVA AT the post office.

But the painter's letter wasn't addressed to Paris—or to anywhere in France. It was addressed, as always, to his wife in Denmark.

Then he saw, underneath her pearly little nails, a letter *from* Paris. His dealer's handwriting. A snail started to unfurl in the painter's intestines.

"You from Paris?" Elva inspected him again. He was covered with red this time—dried, cracked bits everywhere that wouldn't separate from the cloth. Hardened under his nails. A stiff, wide streak of it on his neck.

He nodded. He wanted to be away from her perfect hands. He wanted chowder from the fish shop and a bath and then, fortified, several quiet minutes with the words he'd received from home.

"*Mett*-ee," said Elva, returning her eye to the envelope he needed to send. "Pretty name."

"Mette," he said, letting the T cut flat.

"Your wife?"

"*Ma femme*," he said. "How much for the post stamp please?"

When he'd gone, Elva slipped the final letter to the painter's wife underneath the too-taut twine. Nine in all, one for each week he'd stayed so far.

"Rude," said Elva in her large, warm kitchen. "Something awful."

Lizzie wondered again why the Horn Hill house belonged to her cousin and not to her. A house that was built there, not dragged there. As far from Fish Beach as possible. "I don't think he speaks well," Lizzie said. "English."

It wasn't difficult to steam the new letter open, and the state of the envelope (a grease stain, a smear of red paint where the heal of his hand had pushed in) would make it easy to reseal. Just in case, said Lizzie, the letters had to be mailed someday.

"Biscuit with your chowder?" said Elva.

Lizzie nodded, then tugged a loose thread of the fine lace tablecloth until it snapped. *"Mon épouse,"* she read. *"My wife."* She translated some, but not all, for her cousin.

"Arrange for our kind dealer to meet me at La Havre, as my return passage is now booked for October. I will ship two paintings home beforehand, strong pieces. You'll get 1000 krone a piece, I am sure. Less would be an insult. And unacceptable."

"Krone?" said Elva.

Her bun had loosened as she stirred, red wisps falling down around her pasty face.

"So you see," Lizzie read, *"this trip has been productive. You would find the island dull and provincial, but I have come to care quite a bit for its inhabitants—broad-hipped, foul-mouthed though they may be."*

"Calling the kettle black!" said Elva.

Lizzie took a long sip of too-hot tea.

"The commerce of the mainland doesn't touch them. Or it touches only a little. They know the business of the sea and the tides and have built their lives around this. It's enough for them. One, the Canuck Pastor, still has a supply of ale and absinthe in his cellar. I drink him dry and teach him how to speak French properly. The island painters are amateur at best, still concerned with 'connect the dots' and blurry

trees. Their earnestness is to be admired, at least. They have built little galleries and sheds along the main road here and the day-trippers poke themselves in to buy mementos. But I have saved my best work for Europe. This will please you, I hope."

"Saved where?" asked Elva. "How will we find them?"

Lizzie didn't answer. *"Already I'm thinking of my return to Breton. But that's an argument that can wait for another time.*

"Tell the children I'll bring back enough Indian feathers to stuff ten pillows. I know they'll be excited to see their old Papa. Unless you've already told them that I'm dead."

The cousins ate in silence, thinking. Lizzie swept the crumbs to the floor and pushed the pretty tablecloth aside. She fanned the rest of letters on the lovely, polished table that should have been hers. She read them all again, first to last, as Elva washed up.

> *Dear Mette,*
>
> *I've left you again by having relations with a tall woman from Boston. She smelled like powder, and her waist was half your size. You know I prefer them rounder—I have always wanted a mistress who was fat, and I have never found one. To make a fool of me, they are always pregnant...*

> *Dear Mette,*
>
> *On the cliff today I had to go behind the bush to relieve myself. It has been so long since I—*

Dear Mette,

Please tell the children their father is indeed a savage: I'm fucking the fishmonger! She smells just as you would imagine. And always, always, I think of you…

Lizzie's insides clenched again, reading it. This part she hadn't translated for Elva.

"How much in dollars?" her cousin asked. She turned from the sink to keep Lizzie's gaze.

Lizzie quickly divided. Then divided again.

"And you know where the paintings are?"

"I'll find out," Lizzie said. Then Elva wiped her hands and brought the sherry from the cellar. They ate two doughnuts each before Elva corked up the bottle again.

On the dark road home Lizzie practiced: *Ou sont les peintures, abruti?* At least her shit-for-brains Canuck of a husband had left her something.

So where are they, Frenchie?

12

THE PAINTER SAT ALONE in his room and read quickly. *"Why haven't you written to your wife yet?"* the dealer asked. *"Nine weeks and not one letter?"* It was getting very hard to come up with acceptable Polynesian anecdotes to tell her, he said. He was in Paris to sell some work. And to see the whores, the painter suspected.

"Pola is growing—remember him? Handsome devil but not much heart. Pulls his mother's hair and eats all the sugar straight out of the bowl before she can catch him. He reminds me of his father in every way but one: He replies to her shouting."

The painter folded the paper carefully and burned it in the sink.

He heard Lizzie bang open her door and yell at the girl. No boat shack meeting *ce soir*, it seemed.

So where were all his letters?

13

THE PASTOR ASKED AGAIN. "Will Madame be making the journey?" He watched the painter closely.

"*Non*," said the painter. He shouldn't have come. Lizzie was busy again, and he needed the beer. He rose to use the toilet for the third time, and when he returned, the Pastor looked like he was waiting for an answer still.

"I haven't heard from Madame," said the painter. "Not for an entire summer. *Nine letters* I've written and not one received from my wife. At first I assumed she was angry with me for lying to her. I didn't sail to Polynesia, you see, as I told her I would. But really it's the lack of letters *from me*, though the pigeon lady assures me they've been sent. Madame hasn't received a single one. Why do you think this is?"

They sat at the table in silence, the good wood under their elbows worn and grooved. With the lantern bright between them and the darkness outside, the glass shining back at them, the painter wondered who was watching.

"*Je ne sais pas*," said the Pastor. "It's an island. The mail comes and goes on a shitty little boat. Any number of things could happen."

The painter considered this. He hadn't heard the Pastor say "shitty" before. He closed his eyes to ease the pain in his head and to get rid of the Pastor's glowing face.

As he left, the painter refused a lantern again. "But you'll trip and fall again, no? Easy to do," the Pastor said.

"My eyes are good," the painter answered. "I'd starve otherwise. I have trained them to be good." *Leave me*, he meant. *You should purchase curtains, old man, non?*

His eyes were good. But in the hut in Tahiti he'd had blurry vision for months, the disease spreading from his dick to his eyes. If he slept more, drank less, the doctor had said, his vision would most likely return.

If his daughter hadn't died in Denmark while he'd gone to Tahiti. If his wife had thought to tell him sooner of the coughing. The money gone. The girl's chest raw. Bile, blood, then nothing. If he'd sold the paintings, sent the money. If he'd come back and talked to the bank—

It was God, he'd thought at first. At long last speaking to him. Punished for all this foolishness with paints and tramps.

But then his vision returned. Not because he'd followed the doctor's advice but because he began to have sex with the young girl in his hut again. The black thing that had clamped down behind his eyes opened up again and released him. He was not to be punished after all, even for the death of his daughter. He would see as well as he'd always seen.

It had stopped being the thing he feared most—to be blind. It seemed he'd been granted vision that wouldn't go away.

The painter, *sans* lantern, stopped where the shoreline wet his feet. There was a time when he would have walked in, clothes and all, just to feel something new. The surf was loud, and he couldn't think away the empty feeling the Pastor had brought with his questions.

Lizzie. He thought of her large owl eyes. Lids that drooped, like she didn't believe him. A nose like his own—not an English nose.

Her sturdy jaw. Uncle Turt's stocky pine tree legs. The thick hips, one width from shoulders to thighs. One day he'd borrowed her slicker and hat, left in the closet of his room, went out in the squall to McFadin's, needing a new brush.

A voice behind him had said, "How's the tenant?"

"A little tired. And you?" the painter had answered.

The woman—the island teacher—had blushed. Her son snorted behind the counter.

But to the painter it seemed marvelous. Mistaken for Lizzie! It meant they were similar.

Except he knew Lizzie could throw a man like a fish. Like Mette could. Like she'd threatened to, once. He'd run as far and fast as he could before she'd had another chance.

The painter walked on, away from the shore and up to Graveyard Hill. He needed motion, air—it seemed important to sweat out the badness, which was beginning to stew inside, seep there. He wasn't a fit man, and felt it as he puffed up the slope. He wanted to feel cleaner, just slightly—his pores less acidic. A hike to prepare him for reverie. He'd be glad to reach the place after the steep climb, despite what the ridge contained.

The ground was muddy—he felt his feet sinking in, saw the graves were enclosed only by pines and bushes that someone had trimmed back—no gate, no lock. Just a flat shelf carved out halfway up, the stones planted there. Maybe Captain Smith had decided where it should be: *Good place for the dead, far from the wrecking will of the sea.* The Pastor arranged it now, most likely. Or Vaughan, who had a fine set of shovels lined in his shed. He knew how to cure things, salt things. He could fill the bodies with crystals and let them soak in lime. Vaughan was not a squeamish man. He'd pulled the hook from Lizzie's hand when it caught there deep in the web between her thumb and forefinger. Sucked at the hand hard to get out the rust out—no one wanted to bother with a doctor off island.

Spikes of fish too, in Vaughan's own hand—an infection so severe his finger had turned the shade of a mussel, bluish, almost dead. The Pastor had donated a whole bottle of absinthe to clean it.

All had been revealed in the rowboat.

Lizzie could do the job too—with Vaughan she sliced back gills, scooping them out, those organs that mattered most. Said she looked at her hand slicing the fish sometimes and saw no clear difference between the two, the fishy parts and her own. She had no urge to slice herself, mind you—foolishness. She'd nipped the knife into her own fingers enough times to know it wasn't pleasant. It was just odd that she was the creature cutting instead of the one being cut.

Where was Lizzie now?

The painter coughed into the fog creeping in. Surprising how many stones for such a small island. Tight rows, the names chiseled: Brewer, Barter, Miller, Townsend—orderly, neat. No sign of Turt the house lugger or Lizzie's husband. *Maybe he'd asked for an extra towel too.*

It was a good sign, he supposed, the way the island stones defied the pull of the earth, a final *fu-toi* to death. In Paris the Père Lachaise was rotting, moldy, stones tipped, pushed over by drunks.

His own gravestone was finished, back in Oceania. He'd told Mette—he'd put it in writing and made the dealer serve as witness. Ship his corpse back there, if necessary. He'd be buried in the Marquesas under the statue he'd already carved: *Savage,* it said.

He's morbid, our painter, the dealer had joked in their living room.

He is, Mette agreed. *Excuse me*—and she'd left to tend to Pola.

But it was precisely about his children, the painter told her—it was about maintaining a view of life and death that was not forced upon you! This was the lesson they should learn. Later he'd tried again to explain, cupping her from behind like he used to.

Your children are too young for this, she'd said in Danish, in case they were listening. *They see sketches of headstones and think their father is planning to die.*

Her voice had been cold and even, a plain horizon line. But she hadn't pushed his hands away.

In the island graveyard the light was changing. The painter sat on the wet grass between the stones of Cyrus and Asa. Asa who'd been married to Metty.

Metty? He blinked. The absinthe. *Betty.*

The only cure was more of it—forget the spoon and the sugar cube. It was foul tasting without, but the effect was the same, quicker if anything. He drank, then licked the drop that slid down the length of his mottled flask.

14

LIZZIE WAS NOT IN the rowboat—it was much too late. The house was dead and the lights were out. The painter knocked on the front door anyway.

"Mumma!" he heard inside. The girl padded to the door, eyes mole-like from sleep. She squinted up and said it again: "Mumma! The tenant!"

Lizzie appeared then, bathrobe wound tightly. "Bit too late for a bath, ain't it?"

He waited for the wide smile to follow. It didn't.

"Back to bed," she said to the girl. And then to him, in a hiss so quiet he wasn't sure he'd heard right at first, "'*Mon épouse*'? Don't you ever. Disturb me and my girl again." And then she shut the door, clipping his cap brim.

He waited, then spit out a long sentence in French. He felt steeped in something rotten—absinthe and another kind of liquid inside—but he wasn't too drunk to understand. She knew about Mette, his wife. Because of Elva, the nosy bitch.

He stomped upstairs to his room. Quiet. A black, aching silence. Then small noises below that made him too alert, chest thumping. A drawer slid open and shut. A lock snapped—*a lock?* A sharp whisper from Lizzie: "*Come! Now!*" The soft wail of the girl.

In the morning, out of coffee, he made tea he couldn't drink and then stomped back down to find her, to explain. But the door was already open and the curtains drawn.

She pulled at his hand in her warm kitchen and said, "That wasn't right," she said. "Elva's come by. Took Antoinette for the day."

Who was Antoinette?

"My girl. Took her. I'm not working today."

She looked at him carefully. "I know your kind. I'm like that too." The coffee on the stove was steaming. "Have a bite," she said, and he did. Three whole doughnuts, crumbs in his beard—famished from the night-worry. He stopped the sentences he'd prepared. About how it was with Mette and him.

Then they slept in her bed for the first and last time.

Lizzie was gone for good by nighttime. Gone with the girl to the mainland and from there, who knew? This is what Vaughan told the painter, with a hard-to-read clench in his face. His hands were chapped like mackerels. His eyes were fierce but sorry looking.

15

"COME LATE OCTOBER, I pack up and go," the painter said.

The Pastor stared at his lap. "Back to Europe?"

The painter nodded. Now that he'd exposed his privates to the Pastor, could he tell him everything? His nights in the shack with Lizzie? His daughter, gone? The arsenic he'd taken in the South Pacific? He hadn't had the bad thoughts in a while, the churning, heaving thoughts. Rubbed them out with other liquids, he hoped.

But the fall on the path, Schuff's letter, the fight with Lizzie—all of it had brought something back. A strong, slick ripple toppling all the light and color he'd defined that day. Sickness like a wave that wouldn't crash.

In speaking, maybe it would break a little.

But the silence grew and hardened. *I'm drunker. Much, much drunker than the Father*—and this realization propelled the painter again back into the night without saying anything he wanted to say.

How long had he been on the island? The painter stopped in the middle of the road to count on his good hand, bending the fingers back as far as they would go: May, June, July August, September. Too long—longer than he'd meant to by a full month. How had the island become an enticement? America, even? It was only the dregs of Europe, the ones who couldn't find their way. Misfits and fuck-ups and their minions.

He was late. Mette would worry.

He stayed in the road not moving and kept track of the tiny shifts from not sober to sober, wanting and not wanting them to come. *The stars.* Something to enjoy and pick at for a while. Like a tall piece of corn.

Corn? Mette said.

He meant—the fullness of something there just for him. A buttery kind of gift he didn't feel obligated to paint. *Can we stop it, Mette? Can we make the agreement something else? I'm so very tired.*

She'd understand if he explained, if his letters ever got there. His skin was prickly and hot—he was sweating despite the ocean air, his legs bothered by the wooly fabric of his trousers. He wanted to take them off, to be standing bare in the road, as he'd sometimes done during the hottest weeks in Pont-Aven, as he'd often done in Papeete.

His trousers. The Hairy Baker. The old man sitting in his chair, staring at his lap. Just distraction in the night, all of them just bodies needing friction. Just as Vincent had, rest his soul. Vincent, who'd known the painter well. That summer in Pont-Aven with Vincent.

The painter's breath was loud in his ears. The loose line of a rope *thwapping* against a hull somewhere in the black harbor. The tricky, taunting sea. It never looked right in his paintings. Even with the good easel, it hadn't been right.

Just an easel, *just a thing*, his mother had often said—*just a thing, cher.* When things went missing: books, marbles, the tiny giraffe carved from teak and meant to live inside the bowl-shaped ark. Which was odd because his mother had once liked pretty things, had cared about texture and light and objects well placed in a sunny room.

He missed it. That easel.

We mustn't love objects more than people, she meant. *Things can always be replaced.*

This was before the family fortune had been diverted, before the Peruvian relatives had changed their minds. The painter and his mother returned to Europe with their clothes and two books, Victor Hugo and Hans Christian Andersen. On the long sea trip back from Peru, the boy's mother had pointed to the water and said, "Tell me what you see."

"Blue," said the boy, who hated dumb, obvious questions.

"No," said his mother. "Look closely. What colors are really there?"

The boy looked at the waves for a very long time, remembering the last sea journey, the strangers on deck gathering with blank faces to stand blankly with them. His father's body slipping.

"I see gray," he said. "And very small flecks of white where the waves begin. And black where the shadow of the bow covers the water below."

His mother offered her new, tight smile and said, "You have good eyes."

In the cramped apartment they shared with relatives in Paris, the boy gave a collage to his mother for Christmas—bits of twig and shell shellacked with *mache de papier* onto a board he's found by Sacré Coeur. All his favorite things mashed up and arranged just so. It was hard at first for him to give such a beautiful thing away. But he knew that to hoard his treasures, to let them accumulate, was greedy and foolish.

His mother thanked him, kept the collage on the mantel until New Year's, then smashed the board in two for firewood. The painter had tried to keep his expression hidden but his mother only looked past him, past the panes and the street, like she was still looking out to sea.

The painter had decided she was wrong about things being just things. Let her break them, let her have this satisfaction, at least—he would keep making more. He would replace the old broken things with new broken things.

*

In his room, thinking of the old collage, the painter felt a final clutch in his stomach, the quick pulse of the turpentine diffused, the donut crumbs like snowflakes in his lap. He remembered the plate she'd left at the bottom of the stairs—a plate he'd nearly kicked into the sand in his stupor, then polished off in minutes.

A lot of doughnuts in one week, he'd thought. Right there, just for him—waiting on the very bottom step. He'd been forgiven.

16

THE TAILS OF THE Pastor's coat flapped as he watched the sun sink behind the buffer island, a slash of red caught in the hermit's broken widow. Like the light was stuck there.

He'd found the idea of the hermit ridiculous at first: A man sailed all the way from Galway, then stopped at the lesser island? Why not stop at the island proper where at least he could get bread and beer?

The Pastor's bones ached in the cold. Without thinking, he clasped his hands behind him. The posture of a pensive man.

But he wasn't this man, not really. He preferred company to solitary thought. He preferred artists and their loose, smelly ways.

When the painter didn't come for lunch or dinner, the Pastor inquired at the dock, a granny knot beginning to form inside.

"Hard to say," said the boat captain. "Might have been onboard. Awfully crowded last time."

At the post office, Elva just blinked at him, mouth twitching.

At the fish house Vaughan hacked a pogie in two with a long blade. The eyes of the fish were small, hard berries. The Pastor had an urge to pluck them out.

"Maybe he went after Lizzie," said Vaughan. He looked at the hacked up fish. He smelled like beer.

"And where is she exactly?" asked the Pastor.

"Gone off island."

"So you said. Where?"

"Didn't say. Just left. Miss him?"

"Excuse me?"

"Miss the frog?" His eyes stayed focused on the dead thing in his hands.

"I'm asking as his Pastor."

"He go to church much this summer?"

"Good day, Vaughan. I trust you'll let me know if you have any news."

"Good Christian, was he?"

The Pastor flinched; the verb tense struck him. He couldn't help but turn at the door.

Vaughan smirked his odd smirk, his mouth like a hook, his hands smeared. But the Pastor could see there was pain there too—his eyes quite fierce and lonely in saying her name out loud, *Lizzie. Gone.* Something like a plea.

"Good, yes. Christian, I've no idea," said the Pastor.

So Vaughan had seen them through the window, the naked painter and the old, sad man wanting not to be touched by God.

It was more than the fisherman had ever said to him.

The Pastor waited. He didn't ask to borrow the boat; he bailed it quickly, wetting his good shoes, and pushed it into the tide, though it tweaked his back to do so. The distance across the harbor was deceptive but still he hurried, the feel of the oars in his palms a kind of comfort, the rip in the V of his palms something to focus on.

In the shack the smell reached him first. He didn't need to open the trap door to the cooling cellar (where the hermit had apparently stored his vegetables and milk, his occasional bottle of ale), but he did, just to be sure. The body was slumped, folded, the mouth blackened, the bearded face of the handsome Parisian blank as sailcloth.

17

LIZZIE KNEW THERE WAS A place called St. Cloud's upstate. On the Boston and Maine, she slept until afternoon sun cut into her rattling compartment. Under her pillow the long, hard tube was still there, the paintings rolled inside. She dreamed of Vaughan and Elva and her girl Antoinette beneath a pile of fish guts spinning, growing taller, until it was large enough to hide several bodies. Periwinkles and sea fleas working in until the mound became a throbbing, living thing. Not a nightmare, exactly, but not a comforting vision either.

The worst part would come once she got there.

She could stay until the pains came, until the baby was taken. The thin-lipped nurses would assume the father was a savage, an Indian from upstate, one of the angry handful left. *Bastard*, they'd whisper. *Against her will.* How else could the child's skin be so dark? Better the baby should be raised a Christian in a more civilized place.

"I want the baby to speak French, please," Lizzie whispered. She clenched someone's hand. Lewiston, perhaps, where they could find a proper family.

She would leave the dictionary and the letters, wrapped in the ripped sail from a ruined skiff. She wanted the child, at least, to know.

She'd felt the familiar swelling in her breasts and began to plan with Elva in earnest. She'd taken the paintings, having checked the spaces behind the floorboards and the pea coat when she went to change the sheets.

Then Lizzie had a thought while making the weekly doughnuts. Elva didn't have to know right away. She'd stage a fight. *A wife! How dare he!* She'd be loud about it, and so would he. Who would ask if he disappeared? And if *she* disappeared, no one would know where to follow.

She made him a large batch with extra sugar to hide the taste, knew the drunk, pudgy fucker would eat them all in one sitting. That was his way—everything all at once.

That's how Lizzie would live now too.

She sent the girl to stay with Elva and left the doughnuts on the stoop. Told Vaughan exactly what to say. Hid in her house with the lights off and waited.

She heard him take the plate. Then his bare, manicured feet slapped on the rugs her mother had sewn. She heard his kettle boil, his chair scrape.

Then quiet.

So much quiet Lizzie's heart began to clang. What if she hadn't done the proportions right? What if she was stuck in Turt's drafty old house with the frog upstairs for good?

But then it happened—a thud of a body landing, then the chair, overturned. A heave and a crawling sound—

And quiet again, of a very different kind.

One hour. Two, just to be sure. Then she put on her boots and covered him quick with the curtains he'd already stained with paint. Couldn't look at his face—didn't need to, just felt for his heart and knew. Stopped like a broken metal thing inside.

She rowed to the buffer island with the wheelbarrow at the bow, the stars so pretty she felt someone must be speaking to her from up there. *Good job, Lizzie.* Then wheeled him up to the hermit's shack. Dust inside, and seagull shit—enough to block out, for a little while, the pre-rank smell of man no longer alive.

Opened the trap door. Crammed him inside good.

Her body was sweating and heaving but her mind—it was light, humming. Like crazy Turt probably felt when he finally hit the beach. She slept soundly in her own house, the flap of a boat coil clanging like a simple bell at sea.

On the way to the mainland on the mailboat she didn't look back to see the slip of the island fade, didn't need to see her house. She just stood there at the bow looking hard at the humps of land ahead. She would have herself one last adventure.

Elva would be pissed, thinking she'd gone off island for good. And Vaughan would be sad, thinking he'd be stuck there without her.

She'd leave St. Cloud's when she could, go to Portland. She'd find a dealer. She'd bring some money back for Elva and Vaughan to share. By then the painter would be long gone. Back to his wife in Denmark, they could say, just as he'd promised in his letter.

She'd go back for good, with money for the girl. Who wouldn't have to stay there.

Part Two

Love the one you're with.
—Stephen Stills

Pete

New England, 2003

1

PETE LEAVES TOWN FROM time to time because they know him too well. They know his bad habits and his middle name. They know his wife Molly and his son Emmett and they pull over to say these names in the parking lots of Shop N Save and Video City. "*We know where you live, Pecker.*" They mean the sad, pocked driveway and the old, drafty homestead on Townsend Gut. They know that he's from away—from Lewiston, where most people spoke French at one time—and isn't likely to return.

Before he leaves, Pete looks out at the still, frigid cove and imagines Molly's people hacking up the Abenakis and stealing their birch bark canoes. The dirt road is lined with stocky pines, weak sun slanting in. In winter the dirt freezes in random stretches, making tricky planes Pete likes to crack with steal-toed boots. Come April, the ice will be gone and Molly's cousins will dump more gravel. In November, the water will pool and freeze again.

It's the too-dark driveway that makes him want to go. And the tart Lipton tea and white toast with orange marmalade and the same inane greeting from the Townsend-owned Ebbtide, where the waitress already knows Pete wants whole milk, no lemon. From the corner booth the Byler brothers hunch over their Folgers and hash fries, plates streaky with yolk. They squash their watch caps down over their ears and rib him for drinking tea. "Shlater, Frenchie," they say, the "see," "you, "later" apparently too hard to keep apart. "*One day at a time.*"

They jingle the door, and the waitress clucks. They know his grade-school nickname and his DUI record and they won't let it go.

2

THE TOWN IS CALLED Bay Harbor, just in case distracted tourists don't know the sea is coming up soon. Downtown there's a summertime clam shack and a taffy factory. There are hats for sale with fake, dried seagull shit. (White Out, Pete guesses.) There are T-shirts: "Bay Harbor: A Drinking Town With A Fishing Problem." There are seal and puffin sightings on a Harbor Cruise, a Sunset Cruise, a Clambake Cruise and a Reggae Cruise. (Red Stripe in bottles; Jimmy Cliff on a boombox.) There are three bars, yards apart, on the rotting downtown wharf: one for townies, one for tourists, one where both can go. Two are boarded up in the winter.

In summer, the masseuse and aromatherapist come to town and set up shop with a lady who does ear candling. There's a man called Dr. Pan whose CD (lute and drum machine) is sold at Video City. After Columbus Day, the only certified healers on the peninsula are the two town dentists.

In summer, it's customary to stay on the wharf drinking until the head bobs, the vision blurs. Pete's classmates do this still, no one he cares to see. On the wharf the summer kids talk about kegs and Squirrel Island, whose parents have gone to Nantucket and for how long. There are many pervy limericks about Nantucket. Pete helps the Boston Whalers tie up at the town landing and watches the summer girls—their shiny hair, their loose, cable-knit sweaters in colors likely to stain (salmon and stone). Tiny gold hoops in their ears, two or three on each side.

Pete wears his chamois shirts tucked in. (Brick red, pine green.) He asks Molly to iron his jeans and his mother to trim his hair. His bootlaces, up close, contain a dozen different flecks of braided brown. (Hound's-tooth?) Hunting boots. He went hunting only once.

But there's hunting, in fall. There's candlepin bowling, year-round. There are pick-up games at the Y and after-school programs listed with exclamation points in the *Bay Harbor Tribune*. There are monthly historical society meetings about smelting and ice harvests. There's a stoplight and a Small Mall with a bank, a Laundromat, and a liquor store. ("Everything you might need," Molly tells her husband.) On the lawn of the two-room library, the two town homeless snooze. They nod when they see Pete's rusted Subaru. They've always been homeless, as far as Pete can tell.

*

As a boy Pete had spells sometimes, just like that girl in the Ben Folds song—*She had spells where she lost time*. That's what his mother called them, spells. As Pete grew up he thought of them as moments cast upon him by small forest creatures, gnomes or Smurfs. He'd spent time in the woods, gathering pine cones for wreathes his mother sold, building lean-tos and fairy houses until his father howled at him to quit it and come in to wash his hands.

Things got dark inside. Pete slept too much, even when cartoons were on and his mother said he could watch until noon. He felt a gnawing first, a rising up and a sinking down. It reminded him of *Moby Dick*, a book his father had started reading at bedtime and wouldn't get to finish. (Later, Pete's own son would like the whale part in *Finding Nemo*, the waves gathering inside the mammoth, fishy ribs.) A whale could swallow a creature whole, even a creature as large as a man, and the man could live in the belly unharmed.

At eight, Pete realized he was whale-like inside. He'd swallowed another boy by mistake and the boy had to keep living in the pit of him, waiting to be expelled.

Pete's father called it spoiled-brat behavior but his mother wanted a second opinion. When they moved to Bay Harbor without Pete's father, Pete's mom took him to see Dr. Lewis, who believed in the balm of the outdoors. Philadelphia had been one great swirling mass of stress—good for business but bad for the digestive track. Better to live full time in Maine. The Way Life Should Be.

Dr. Lewis agreed to take Pete for a walk at Oven's Mouth. He found a pack of American Spirits in the glove compartment and offered one.

"No thanks," said Pete.

"I was ten when I started," said the doctor. He talked about the Yankees and marched ahead. He encouraged frequent masturbation, which made Pete wonder where they were heading.

But when the trail reached Cross River, Pete could see the prehistoric-looking banks of trees, the cliffs jutting above. The small, reluctant ripples on the blue green surface, the rock face unchanging—haggard, gray granite chipped by glaciers, the doctor said.

This part of the peninsula didn't require Pete's interaction, didn't care about his insides at all.

"How'd it go?" asked his Mom. "You smell like cigarettes."

"He smokes," said Pete.

She frowned. "I suppose he's not a real doctor."

Pete didn't see Dr. Lewis again, but later he biked to Oven's Mouth on his own, mainly to walk, sometimes to do the other thing Dr. Lewis suggested behind a large blackberry bush. He liked the exertion and the quiet, the unlikelihood of the whale appearing there.

"Going to Grover's," he said to Molly a decade later.

"What?"

"Hardware. Errand." Which meant he was going to Oven's Mouth. He hadn't taken Molly to see the jagged rocks, not once.

"Can you get milk?"

"At Grover's?"

She sighed. "Two percent, please."

It was a test. She must have guessed he wasn't going to Grover's.

He thought he could hide the whale from Molly, but it was hard. She was patient at first, then less so. She saw the blowhole. A swishy flash of tail. She must have.

In bed, Molly sometimes worried about Emmett out loud and Pete tried not to hear her. *I hope he'll turn out right*, she said. Which meant, she hoped to god he didn't have it too.

*

The idea was that Pete would paint and look after Emmett. Molly would work at the bank. He could sell his work in summer, and they'd use the money for trips to Paris, to Amsterdam, where hash was sold in the supermarkets, Pete had heard.

But after high school, after the boatyard fired him for borrowing too many misshapen planks, Pete got a job at the lobster pound where Molly's cousins and uncles came to dump their catch. He didn't fudge the numbers, and so they called him Tightwad or Frenchie the Jew. He tolerated the bait smells, the aches from unloading. He grew his hair longer. He wore gloves to keep his hands from getting too hard.

But the hours suited him. He could paint at night, lock himself in the basement with the radio on. He could show up tired or high and no one seemed to care.

He thought, briefly, about applying to be the art teacher, K through 8. But the thought of more classes made the whale tail flap.

Molly had gone instead. Two years at University of Southern Maine and she'd been at the bank ever since.

She said Pete should use her old gingerbread shed, take out the shovels, the garden hose, dismantle the ancient wasp's nest glopped on the roof.

"You could paint in there," said Molly. "Or Em might take to it later."

"Doubt it," said Pete. It was a girlie thing, curly white trim against cheap, red-slapped pine. Built too late for the kind of play Molly's parents had in mind.

"It should be properly utilized somehow," his wife said to him.

Pete looked away. She did that—used longer words when simpler ones would do.

"You'd be outside. Daylight coming in. Turn on the space heater and what not. Could be quite cozy in there."

But it smelled like mouse shit, and she'd written things on the walls: *I Heart Simon Le Bon's Awesome Ass*, *I Heart New York*, which she'd revised: *I Have Mixed Feelings About New York*.

She'd brought Flip Johnson there, his long legs jerking around on the creaky burlap cot, his own awesome ass clenching.

He'd noticed how men had looked at her intently, especially that one time in New York, the Art Club trip, men with kind smiles and floppy hair and men with piercings in places other than their ears. During long hours at the pound he ached with a phantom jealousy, thinking about it still. She'd smile while talking. She'd laugh and touch their hands in Strand Books or Tower Records. How easy to slip into something new with a man who didn't smell like fish.

For this reason he sometimes didn't follow her, didn't obey. Meet me *here*, Molly said at the Maine Mall or the Portland Civic Center when they parted to use the bathroom or get snacks—before cell phones, when they had to stick to these kinds of plans to find each other again.

He didn't stick. He stayed fifty yards off the mark, feigning absorption in T-shirt vendors. She'd have to think hard about what he was wearing that day. *The red chamois or the green?*

"Why?" she said when she found him again. Her forehead was tight. "Why do you do that?"

He shrugged, meaning, *Didn't mean to,* and slung an arm around her neck to make her forget.

He liked to see the quick rush of relief before she got pissed. He could pretend she was fifteen again and he knew exactly who she was: Molly Townsend, Class President, daughter of Will and Val. Beer drinker. His girl in the car on the rocks with the sounds of the waves crashing through.

She'd chosen him. He tried to keep remembering this.

*

It was Molly, not the Ebbtide waitress, who got Pete started on tea, tureen-like mugs of it with heated milk, Emmett not yet born. Because of Molly, Pete could soon tell the difference between English and Irish Breakfast, between Earl and Lady Grey. When she brought in the mugs she made him guess, her big, boxy ass showing under a too short T-shirt—Huey Lewis or Hall and Oates, awful bands they'd seen together in Portland.

Part of the ritual was the clutching of the bowl, warming up slowly from the inside. It made the tongue less acidic and the bowels less full. Unlike the chemical shock of coffee. "Nice," Pete said. "*Bowels.*" But she was right. Weekends they drank several cups in bed, the nubbed flannel sheets around them, the sun quiet between the blinds. They took turns filling the kettle and then leaned against the headboard, sipping and not talking, feet touching.

When she went to refill, Pete said *don't leave me* because he didn't want to go to the basement. If they just stayed like that, waking carefully, he wouldn't have to go.

But she left. The day had to begin.

He ordered things from the Victoria's Secret catalog and hoped she'd retire the T-shirts. He wrote, in a tiny pink card, *Really like your peaches, wanna shake your tree.* He made himself stop and cool down, made himself get up to pee. And then he was ready again, and she was still there on the spread from Pier One her parents had bought them, little mirrors the size of quarters glued on blue cloth. She didn't seem too tired, though he sensed, sometimes, when she dug in her fingertips and started breathing faster, that she wanted him to hurry up and be done.

Then it shifted. She said she shrunk the fancy negligee. She began to nudge him away, reading. She needed something to read to wake up and besides, all that lounging made her feel itchy, sloth-like. Then Emmett came and there was no time even for that.

He read a little from a novel she'd left open, a story about an Old West woman living in a place called Mineral Palace. He caught the phrase "finite use" and something budged inside as he read on. It was about having a finite use for someone, using a person between periods of badness or confusion or loneliness.

He wondered if she'd left it out for him to see. His finite use for her? Her finite use for him.

3

THIS TIME, PETE LEAVES because it's November and Emmett just turned three. After toast and tea at Ebbtide, after tipping the waitress poorly, Pete snaps the Subaru's heat dial to red. He waits to hear three songs on commercial-free BLM (two when one happens to be "Hotel California"), then lets the blower gust the ready warmth around. He takes the back way, pauses to scan the shitty driveway, blows a kiss for Molly and Emmett to share.

He doesn't nod to Jared Pinkham, whose roof rack is still bent from the rollover, or to Byler Sr., his truck bed crammed with lobster traps in need of repair. He grips the cold steering wheel. He drives the swervy length of the peninsula, deciding not to stop, not even to pee, until he gets to Old Orchard Beach. Like the crazy ex-astronaut, the one who wore diapers as she sped across states to murder her cheating boyfriend. He remembers the mockery, David Letterman and something about Pampers. But Pete gets it. She just had to keep driving, the astronaut. She had to do the completely insane thing. She'd feel bad about it, but later.

Things press down on Pete's lungs. A watery feeling, like a lack of gills. Further away will be better. He needs a different kind of sea air.

There are closer beaches—Reid State, Popham—but Pete doesn't care for them. At Old Orchard the water will be steely and the rides will be shut, the imprint of people having yelled in the sun many months before. He blasts the heat and tries to be there already.

4

PETE REMEMBERS THE SWINGING ax of the Pirate Ship, how sure he'd been it would fly all the way around, dumping him on the cracked boards of the pier. His parents held hands then and let him have an entire spool of cotton candy, blue threads dissolving like Pop Rocks, but safer. (He'd wanted a candy apple, but his father reminded him of the Common Ground Fair and said *No*—the too-big bite, almost half the apple gone, the slice of plastic-y red lodged in Pete's throat, the pig manure smell making everything taste like butt.)

At Old Orchard, they'd been surrounded by other Canucks. (It was okay for Pete to say this.) His parents spoke in whole, gurgling paragraphs that swooped in—everyone talked that way on the pier. It was hard for Pete to push into his parents' words, and he was glad he didn't have to. He saw at Old Orchard how his mother and father might be a pair that fit.

But on the way back to Lewiston, the sun fading, they'd wanted him to join them in dialogue.

"What do you see out there, Petey?" His mother turned to face him. Her eyes were bright green, a sea shade. She looked happy and sunburned. She slid the radio dial down to listen.

Speak. At school Pete's teacher said they'd run out of words if they talked too much. He meant the noisy ones, but it made

Pete feel better. He should save his words, keep them safe in the pit of him. He swallowed them. It was such an effort to force the thoughts up, belly to throat to lips. He practiced inside his head, took his time with choices and order. He sometimes remembered them later, sentences perfectly formed but unspoken.

From the back seat he saw a tree limb, snapped and limp like a broken neck.

"Is that so," said his father. "Let someone else get a word in." His father did this, abrupt jokes to change the mood. His mother laughed. She'd had two frothy drinks on the pier.

It was so much easier to look at things. Pete liked to take in segments of color and light, forcing the rush of roadside to settle. He tried to make his eyes stay fixed on each blurred thing: the number plate on a telephone pole, a red mailbox with a streak of black lettering, a chimney spitting one fine plume. He began to spot things in the woodsy stretches between houses: a tall woman praying in a long white cloak, a wild boar with yellow teeth, a human head torn and left behind.

But the small radio whine was all his parents could hear. "Your mother is asking," said his father.

What did he see? "I see a wild boar," he said, knowing the broken neck would require too many words.

"He's just tired," said his mother, and nudged the volume up again.

Pete knew he was right about the things in the woods because of Stephen King movies. It would be easy to bump into something, get snatched and chopped, which could happen when he got kindling from the stack under the porch, or raked their bumpy lawn, or called Maisey in at night, until she got hit by a car. There were rules, though. The creatures weren't everywhere. A Puritan know-how kept them from mucking about in places with too many churches or where families were loving and tight.

"Masshole," his father said to the passing car. His mother snorted. Someone from away, someone not giving a shit about the rules.

Much later, when Pete finally looked at a map, he was surprised to see how close they were to Massachusetts, only a strip of dull New Hampshire in between.

Pete didn't remind his father they'd been from away once too. All his old Quebecois relatives still had the accents to prove it.

Pete had a wispy memory of bad smells: farts and disinfectant in a room that needed air. The cave of his great grandfather's chest beneath a ballooning button-down shirt. Pete begged to leave minutes after they arrived and his mother shushed him. This was her relative, her grandfather, an orphan who'd grown up to live a long time. His mother spoke to him in French, shouting to make the old man understand, and Pete held his breath as long as he could.

He seemed to be shedding right in front of the boy. Fake teeth left on the dresser. Dandruff in his eyebrows. A strange white cowlick no one bothered to comb away. But his eyes were bright, a little wicked.

"We have to respect these people, our elders," she explained to Pete as they drove away from Sunny Hills. "An orphan. Can you imagine?" She reached behind to touch the tip of an old manila envelope, peeking out of her purse.

In his childhood room in Lewiston, while his parents watched *MASH*, Pete drew shapes on a yellow pad. When they were right, he left them out for his mother to see.

He'd memorized the Crayola names: burnt sienna, midnight blue—it *was* midnight blue. It was how the sky looked in summer when the moon was there, dimming blue into purple-black. He'd fought over the midnight crayon with his cousin in Lewiston, and it was the first to be worn down. He'd nibbled on it once, hoping the color would taste like midnight too. It hadn't, but Pete was pleased with himself for trying. Brave with the waxy stuff on his tongue.

Pete had thought he might like that job, coming up with those crayon names. But his mother said it wasn't a job anymore, now that all the colors were done.

In Bay Harbor without his father, Pete began to keep track of license plates in the summer. He'd printed the list alphabetically, asked the school librarian to copy the blank sheet for next year. In the summer of '84, he saw forty-eight, all but Alaska and Hawaii.

"Saw Kentucky today," his dad reported on the phone.

"It only counts if I see it," said Pete. He wondered why someone from Kentucky would even want to come to Maine.

He kept the list unpocked, tacked to his bulletin board, careful to return the pin to the very same hole.

At school they had to memorize the states and capitals and Pete got a 98, just because he mixed up Kentucky with Kansas. They had to memorize the European countries and capitals after, just the western ones. It stopped with Czechoslovakia, which made no sense. A map with so many empty places left to fill in.

He got a camera for Christmas and forgot about the list. His mother called it "making pictures" instead of "taking pictures," and this seemed right. Pete stood in the woods, fixing the light and trees. He propped his favorites between two tacks to avoid holes completely:

1) Squirrel tracks. (Blue sky, white snow, soft indentations of feet leading out.)

2) A close up of sumac in a field where everything else was dead. (The rouged clumps like soft little antlers.)

"You have a wonderful eye," said his mother, balancing the pictures on her palm.

She went back downstairs for more wine.

"Sumac is Camus backward," said his father.

"What's Camus?" Pete yanked the length of the phone cord, wondering if it would snap.

"A very unhappy man," said his father. "But a very good writer."

Camus was like Kentucky. Years later, when Ms. Patrick assigned *The Stranger* in Senior English, Pete skipped it and suffered the D.

His mother gave him the *Griffin and Sabine* books, which were not at all girlie. Pete studied the tiny lines and curls of the imaginary stamps, the actual envelopes with actual letters to pull out and read. It was evidence of a mind like his own. Someone else taking time with the way things looked, even if those things weren't real.

He'd been ten when they moved, and there was a lot to catch up on at Bay Elementary: the boys who'd had lice, the girl who set fire to toilet paper, the boy who'd let one rip in Home Ec, the girl with period blood on her pink satin gym shorts, the boy whose father went to prison, the older sister who sold Oxy, the brother who died in a car crash, the other brother, whom everyone had to be nice to, the nickname for the math teacher, which was Uni-Ball, the boy who'd come up with that name, the boy with a hickey on his butt, the girl who'd probably given the hickey, the girls who'd probably give blowjobs later on, but not the boys who'd receive them.

Pete understood there was no need to advertise the French thing. He watched the half-Jewish boy and the half-Vietnamese girl, who sat alone at lunch until they sat together. She let him drink her Sprite; he dumped her tray. Then everyone let them be.

In Math, Pete sat next to Campbell, the principal's son, christener of Uni-Ball, who unzipped a secret flap in his duffel and withdrew an actual Black Book. In it, he'd rated girls in class in ten categories, including boobs and athleticism. Molly Townsend was the only one to score perfect tens. In the "notes" section, in surprisingly delicate print, Campbell had written, "Really Big Mamas" and "I'd choose her first for teams."

The lowest score went to Lacey Reynolds, whom Campbell called Chewbacca or Chewie.

"Carpet chewer," said Campbell.

Pete said nothing.

"You know. Lezbo."

"How do you know?" This was before he'd learned not to ask.

"She held hands with Rachel Skinner at the Y dance."

"Rachel Skinner's a Chewie?"

She was not. She'd already French-kissed an 8th grader named Ronnie. She wore tight acid-washed jeans and carried Binaca in her backpack, which Campbell said was proof.

Molly Townsend, meanwhile, had a reddish perm hairsprayed into neat, corn chip-shaped curls. Her yellow L.L. Bean pullover was new; she had older ones in violet and red. Her Tretorn sneakers were a neutral navy blue.

If Pete had his own Black Book he'd write, *Family owns half of town; Rear I'd like to fondle.* When she smiled, her cheeks pierced in on themselves like awl notches in fresh white pine.

But then she danced with Flip Johnson to "Faithfully" by Journey. She never said no at dances. It was the last song of the night—it was always the last song of the night—and Flip did a little yelp of recognition when it came on. (It may have been his tape.) He wore Air Jordans and parachute pants, which Pete had longed for. His hair was spiked into sharp-looking points. He was taller than everyone in class. He was taller than Uni-Ball.

Pete watched them circle and laugh until he couldn't anymore and then went to drink beer in Campbell's car.

In eighth grade Pete was allowed to skip the bus and walk to Cutting Edge after school, past McSeagull's and the quiet row of dories. The air was salty and the water was black; the footbridge boards creaked. Pete counted as he crossed and lost track at 103.

The two other stylists at Cutting Edge were married to Millers and had matching feathered cuts. They tolerated his mother, who at least was not a hippie. The previous perm girl, a distant relative who needed a job, wore braids and thick sandals. She complained about the chemicals and discouraged clients from getting treatments. She quit to join the Peace Corps in Hondurus, where she contracted dengue fever, exactly the sort of thing that happened when grooming went by the wayside, said the Miller women.

There was a tanning bed like a plastic coffin, so Pete lay down and lowered the lid. He wasn't allowed to turn the tanner on, but he wore the little oval goggles and listened as the same Lionel Ritchie songs looped on the boombox. Through the coffin slot he could see the poster of Hawaii, the aqua waves just about to crash into a lean and carefree surfer. He could see, jutting out of the wall like logs, two *faux* Corinthian columns painted dark peach (or nougat?) with hollowed-out flutes. The Miller husbands had constructed them from plaster after looking at a picture of the Parthenon.

Pete knew about the flutes because he had a book at home, *Jansen's Art History*, sent from his Grammy in Lewiston. He knew about cornices, dentils. He knew the sea wasn't really blue, but many combinations of gray and green and purple. It was a million colored lines jumping all at once.

He couldn't yet copy the sea, which was a difficult thing to accept. On weekends, he rode his bike to Ocean Point and drew until the tides started to change. He peed behind a rock. He imagined taking Molly there and wondered if she would mind peeing behind a rock. He thought some more about how and where she might pee and this made him have to pee again. He felt walled in by these thoughts at the Point, pleasantly surrounded. His pad, his pencils, the impossible shades of water.

Then someone honked—someone his mother knew or someone from school with a shotgun rack. "Frenchie!" He nodded. He closed his sketchpad. He smoked the Camel he'd stolen from his mother's pack.

When he wasn't drawing he was making mobiles out of bent spoons and bracelets from bottle caps. He stenciled dolphins on his mother's flowerboxes and began to cover the hood of her old Mazda with epoxy and pennies. She seemed glad about these projects. She asked her customers to dump their coins in a Pringles can by the register.

He tried to draw the summertime storefronts, made them cheery and crowded: The Hutch, Tigger Leather, Sherman's Books, Orne's Candy, The Smiling Cow, Christmas Corner, Mountain Top Tees.

His mother hung it on the wall right by Hawaii, and even the Miller girls said he had a gift.

At fourteen, Pete got a work permit like everyone else and a summer job at the boatyard on the East Side. The kids who were fourteen and didn't have work permits were lazy or rich or both. Or they'd been working on their dads' lobster boats for years already.

It wasn't just for money, said Campbell; it was a way to get invited to the parties on Squirrel Island. You'd work with summer kids, whose parents made them pay for Boston Whaler fuel and new Tevas. They went to Philips Exeter or Hebron Academy instead of Bay High. Pete could see that the names of their schools meant something to adults. Better to flunk out of Hebron than to spend four years at Bay Harbor.

Pete didn't go to many parties but he liked having the money from the boatyard, which he spent on oil paints and brushes. He had to go to Wiscasset to get them, a small shop called *Les Couleurs*. His mother drove him on weekends.

He didn't let anyone see, but he was proud of his latest painting in a way he'd been proud of the sumac photo.

It was a painting of Molly, of course. He'd taken his time with it. He'd felt a little funny and a little horny, shading her skin on the page.

Fall came again. The stairwell in Bay Harbor High was bird's egg blue. The stairs were like a ship's quarters, like the space between decks, the metal ringing from the stream of thudding feet between classes. Pete could see the uneven bumps from the long-ago brush and knew if he dug in a thumbnail he could peel a scabby bit away, leaving a small metal patch. He didn't do this though. He tried not to touch railings—as a rule he tried not to touch anything a lot of other people had touched.

He went to Chemistry because Molly was there. He sat two rows in front of her and tried not to slouch.

In the hall, the French teacher spoke to Pete as various relatives from Lewiston had, with tobacco breath and spittle, gnarled hands clenching. Pete caught, in French, "please tell your mother" and then went to Shop II, a class filled with juniors and seniors, a place where no one spoke much. Pete liked the sawdust smell, the jagged tools, the need for goggles. He liked the whir of the planer, which he could use without asking. He made necklaces out of leftover solder for the Cutting Edge ladies and plexiglass sunglasses in blue, yellow and red—short wooden dowels for frames. When Mr. Farley left for cigarette breaks, Pete slid sheets of new sandpaper into his notebook.

This interest in shop pleased his father, who still managed the car dealership in Lewiston. His father seemed proud of a lot of things Pete did, now that he was married to someone else.

Then Campbell was caught with pot. It was a big joke, his dad being the principal. He'd been caught before—the cans of Bud at dances, the little Black Book. In the Y lot, he threw the rest of it at Pete, a plastic baggie tucked under and half-full. Pete thought of the carrots his mother used to pack in baggies. String cheese sometimes.

"Ass-face is searching my room every day," said Campbell. "I could get fifty bucks for it. Want it for ten?" He wore expensive-looking sunglasses, the Tom Cruise kind.

"Better not," said Pete. He could smell the funk in the bag. He looked around at the brown snowdrifts, the foggy glass doors of the pool entrance. Muffled shouting of parents at small breaststrokers. "Where they sending you?"

"Hebron," Campbell said. "Maybe Choate."

"Shit," said Pete. "For smoking the bowl?" Smoking *the* bowl?

"Whatever." Campbell leaned back against his truck, his throat pale. "I'm taking faggoty French. Probably speak it better than you." He smiled like Tom Cruise and got in his truck. "Cold as Ice" came on and a wet little boy in goggles opened the pool door to see.

That night, behind a rock at the Point, Pete plucked a Camel half empty with his mother's tweezers and filled it with Campbell's weed. He smoked until his chest felt too full, until he was aware of his own organs, working hard.

In the summer he bought a bong at the new age store, where whale music blared, where Molly worked. He paid in cash and watched her pretty hands make change. She said she couldn't stand the incense smell—sandalwood and jasmine shit—which she had to burn all day. (Once they were married, incense was banned.) She had to make sure no one stole the crystal pendants or the tarot cards. She kept the curtain drawn over the bong closet.

On a Saturday in August he picked her up after work and drove to the Point, where they tested his purchase together behind the rocks. He told her about the painting and she asked when she could see it and when they kissed it was like the ocean was everywhere, inside and out. She didn't have to pee so Pete didn't have to worry.

Junior year they went to New York City with the Art Club after selling a lot of cupcakes and brownies. Or, the rest of the Club did this. Pete bought and sold some weed. They saw the Met and the MOMA and were supposed to stay at a YMCA in Chinatown, which the art teacher, Ms. Barker, had promised was perfectly safe.

Pete and Molly never found out if the Chinatown Y was safe—after the MOMA, they took the mushrooms Pete had been saving and crossed the Williamsburg Bridge, back and forth. They went to Alphabet City and took pictures with Molly's Polaroid. They saw a man hunched over a fire hydrant with a syringe stuck in his thigh and men in the bushes of Tompkins's Square Park, their pants at their ankles. "It's like something from *National Geographic*," said Molly.

"Since when do you read that?" said Pete.

As Molly waited in line for free plates of food from Hare Krishnas, Pete saw a woman staring down at him from several stories. She was topless—naked, maybe. (What had the New Yorkers done with all of their clothes?) The window frame cut just below her waist. She wasn't leering. She just seemed intent on making Pete look back.

Apart-ment, he realized. Little homes stacked high and separate. He waved. She closed the window and ducked away.

New York City! Here you could make a mistake and no one would remember or care. No one would call you a queer the next day.

Molly came back with dripping plates, and he kissed her hard. "I want to fondle in the bushes. Can we?"

They could not, she said. She was hungry. It wasn't safe.

They walked to Canal Street instead, just as the light began to nudge itself into day. They boarded the bus that would take them back to the place they'd lived all their lives.

In the back, Pete reached under the long, gauzy flap of Molly's skirt and rubbed and rubbed as the rest of the Art Club dozed, until she clenched and sighed and fell into his lap. His leg went numb and he jiggled it a little, trying not to wreck her sleep.

He was thinking of the way the buildings looked in late afternoon. A slate of color, a spotlight. He could paint that. He knew what it felt like. Heat warming brick after a long, damp morning in shadow.

Soon after, Pete built a houseboat near Lobster Cove, where he could hide and float away in the dark. He'd borrowed the abandoned pieces of hull from the shipyard and hid them under a tarp. He'd carved the fiberglass floats with a borrowed jigsaw, wood-burned "MT" at the aft. Then he launched the thing, took Molly there. Carried her through the mudflats at low tide. She was heavy and he said so and she laughed at this, a bottle of Riunite tucked under her armpit.

The officer didn't come until morning, Officer Dicky Roy, uncle to Abbot Roy, one year behind them in school. *Private property*, he said, *no permit for the thing*. He winked at Pete and got a good look at Molly's bare thighs, where the wool blanket had fallen away.

*

In the fall after graduation, Pete's mother was at Cutting Edge every day and Molly was at college. He looked up the Fauvists and the Symbolists in the *Jansen* book. He copied Matisse and Van Gogh. He traced the starry night circles in black and then blue and black and then blue until it began to mean nothing and everything at the same time. He tried to see how stoned he could get.

Molly finished college early, they got married, and in the basement of the Townsend house, it was pretty much the same. He came to bed smelling like sweat and beer. When he woke on weekends Molly had done the dishes and taken Emmett to the lake for swimming or the pond for skating.

Then, for his birthday, she bought him a book by a famous painter, a collection of letters and tirades against colonists called *The Writings of a Savage*. Something Pete's mother had recommended. Pete found a red pencil and underlined the quotes he liked best. He looked at Molly again because of the book. She understood him a little. She was willing to accept what he'd become.

The frontispiece was a print of Gauguin's "Where Do We Come From? What Are We? Where Are We Going?"

Pick up lines, Pete had thought. Past, present, future. A way to make someone stay a little longer. *Where you from? What do you do? What are you doing later?*

He could do his fieldwork at the Thistle Pub. A new project, like pennies on the hood of his Mom's car.

Paul. No one in his class had that name. *Paw. Paw-l.* The mouth had to draw itself out, down. Fishlike. Like a yawn that could lead somewhere else.

5

LIKE OLD ORCHARD BEACH. Pete hits I-95 South and reaches into the glove compartment for his baggie. "Oh Sherrie" comes on and he changes the station. The thoughts keep arriving in MTV fragments, a stream he can't control. He rubs at his crotch a little and turns down the Subaru heat.

How willing Molly used to be, with her teeth stained purple. In a houseboat that was leaky and cold.

It isn't Molly. It's the tea and toast at Ebbtide. The fucking Bylers and everyone they know.

It is Molly. And Emmett, some.

He sometimes watched them from outside the picture window, before coming inside, Molly stirring and feeding. She turned lights off in one room and on in another and didn't sit down. How efficient she was. A calm could seep in, despite her duties. She was a still, plum sky about to burst.

And then it did burst. She screamed over "Jungle Love" as Pete, shirtless, continued to streak reds over the fine, gray lines he'd sketched. He turned up the tape deck. She kicked the basement door shut.

"What's wrong?" Emmett asked later.

"Nothing, bub." Pete made strange noises and lifted his son from the rug to make him forget.

At those times he'd wished for normal pleasures—football or darts. People asking chatty kinds of questions.

He passes the Subaru ahead of him, thinks *Masshole*. But it's a Maine plate.

He remembers the *Book Of Questions*, which Molly brought to the Point and read by the light from the radio: *Is it okay to kill one man in order to save many? Is it better to be deaf or blind?* That one made Pete jumpy. He was supposed to say deaf—he needed his eyes. But maybe, if he just didn't have the option, everything would be better, more peaceful. He'd be forced to give up on sight.

Molly said deaf, because then she wouldn't have to hear him go on and on about his fucking paints anymore. Then she kissed him and peeled off her sweatshirt in the dim, lovely night.

They'd given up on him a little, Molly and Em. At four the boy knew to do this, shifting his eyes to his mother when Pete came into the room. His son. A very small housemate. Just a temporary arrangement until he found a place of his own. Was that cruel?

He'd worried about the name. Emmett. Molly had picked it at St. Andrew's, sweat matting everything on her. *From inside the dictionary*, she kept saying. He had no idea what she was talking about, until later. She meant his French-English dictionary, handed down.

"Emmett sounds like a girl's name," Pete said to her. Couldn't help saying it.

"Think of our class!" she'd said. "Asa. Calvin. *Cyrus.*"

"Men's names," Pete mumbled. "Old, New Englandy names." Even Peter was risky, a name the Bylers had made synonymous with penis.

"Oh who cares," Molly said. Then she slept for fifteen hours straight.

Emmett's pre-school teacher hadn't used the French pronunciation and it would stick, Pete knew. He would be *Emm*-ett all through grammar school and high school and college. The only one who'd pronounce it right was his grandmother in Lewiston.

Pete called him Em, which *was* girlie. He meant "M," for Molly. Maybe he'd be more like her.

Pete inhales again, rolls down the window a smidge, continues to ignore his bladder. He imagines the plates behind are all from away, summertime cars trailing him, a line of different states in the rearview. His duty to lead them to the prettiest cove.

Then he allows himself, at last, to think of Karla.

6

HE WAS SEVENTEEN, SUMMERTIME. He'd smoked a bowl and walked past the Dinner Theatre, when it was still called the Dinner Theatre. The pretty blonde worked out front in a booth, a summer girl. She said she liked his T-shirt. He thought of the vocab word he'd missed in English. *Effervescent. Like a scent, not a cent.* He wondered how much her clear braces had cost.

But she wasn't a summer girl. Born and raised in Bay Harbor. She'd failed out of Lincoln Academy and would have to go to school with Pete, come fall. Her name was Karla with a K.

He couldn't think of anything clever to say about her name so he shook her hand. She laughed at him.

Too bad Campbell's gone, thought Pete. *The Black Book would be revised.*

The day before Molly came back from Girls' State (some kind of mock Congress she'd been excited about) Karla took him to the tiny cottage on the way to Ocean Point. It was meant to be a summer cottage, but Karla lived there year-round now with her parents and two sisters. Her room was in the basement, mossy carpet on the walls and an orange afghan her aunt had knitted. A record player of her own. She could shimmy out the upper window at night—she showed him how. She pointed to the patch of grass where a Frisbee had knocked out her sister.

Then she came back inside and played side one of *A Chorus Line*, palming the record at the edges. Her eyes were different, her voice brassier. "*Who am I anyway? Am I my résumé?*" She laughed, and her face broke back into herself. Her lips were pouty and her hair was long, honey-colored. And then she was on top of him, the afghan underneath, her hips moving around. She smelled like bread and vanilla.

"That's a French word, résumé," Pete said.

She kissed him with her tongue, and he didn't say anything else. She moved her hips around again, and he came in his jeans by the time "Nothing" had started.

"You can't French kiss for shit," she said when the needle lifted.

She called him Frenchie after that, just like everyone else.

When Molly came back she talked a lot about Flip, who'd been on the same bus for Boys' State. She was going to his swim meet at the Y. Did Pete want to come? He'd asked them both to come. School spirit and all.

No thanks, said Pete. He decided to feel less guilty about the cottage and Karla.

He made props for the musical, which was *Pippin*. Karla was Pippin, and she needed a large, foil spear. On the handle he wrote: *Your hand here*, and she shrieked at him from across the gym when she saw it.

Someone got sick, and he had to be a soldier in the battle scene. He had to learn the dance routine, and then they decided he could sit down for it. He wore a black, scratchy beard. At the cast party—Dr. Pepper and Cheetos in the Home Ec room—she led him to a distant janitor's closet and, beside the damp-smelling bucket and mop, did just what the Binaca girl had been accused of.

Pete's sudden interest in *Pippin* was something Molly couldn't gauge. *Twirlie*, Molly called her, the girl from Lincoln Academy. A Twirlie was something you weren't supposed to be after a certain age.

After *Pippin*, Karla was Eve in *The Apple Tree*, which Pete went to see all three nights. He liked the part where Eve had to name everything and Adam got confused. Karla said pogie instead of plain old "fish," which got a laugh because, two summers before, thousands of flapping pogies had beached themselves in the harbor. They'd rotted slowly, a bad year for tourists. A smell like salted garbage that wouldn't blow away.

Then Karla failed out of Bay Harbor, soon after *The Apple Tree* had its run.

She didn't care, she said. She was going to transfer to a pre-college program in New York called AMDA. Not AADA, but AMDA, the American Musical and Dramatic Academy, because she wanted to focus on Musical Arts. And because, Pete found out much later, she hadn't been accepted by the other one.

Then Flip Johnson asked Pete to paint the Journey emblem on the back of his jean jacket and he said sure, why not. Pete asked for $30 or the equivalent in pot.

Flip offered cash, and Pete brought the jacket to his mother's garage. The denim was faded and torn at the neck and smelled like fried eggs from Flip's weekend job at Ebbtide. (Ha! Nicknamed for flipping eggs. Not the neat, brave dives he performed for the swim team.) In the pockets, Pete found Dentyne wrappers, movie stubs from *Die Hard 2* and *Navy Seals*, and a new silver Zippo. Pete disliked Journey—the shrill confidence of Steve Perry, the too-tight jeans and the hawk-like nose, much like his own. He preferred

CSNY, Dylan. Singers not in half-shirts. But he'd taken his time with the scarab (red and gold) and the space-age letters (blue and white). It looked good. He kept the lighter.

Flip had worn it all through senior year, then gave it to his "fiancée," a girl from Wiscasset no one had met. She returned it, with the ring, once he enlisted.

7

AT OLD ORCHARD THE beach is empty, gray waves choppy and fierce. Pete finds a diner and a round, pretty waitress who doesn't know to bring him milk. She refills his mug with hot water for no extra charge until the tea bag disperses nothing but the faintest Lipton smudge.

He presses his finger against the teabag and draws a cursive K on the placemat with his finger. He feels, through his jeans, a tear in the vinyl seat.

He refuses to feel like a turd.

He sees Karla on her ship, the picture in the *Tribune: Local dancer/singer cruises the world.* Feathers and heels, wide smile like a mask.

Of course she ended up at sea. The skeletal hulls at the boatyard, the Windjammer Days in June, the bay filled with Whalers—none of it belonging to them, the townies, but still. It was hard to ignore the vessels everywhere.

She'd sent the first postcard from San Juan, care of Cutting Edge. His mother had freed it from the mirror's lip and frowned. Pete was married by then.

"Give it here," he said.

"Putting it on your fridge?" His mother's hair was a new, startling shade of rust.

"Jesus. It's a postcard."

"She's a flirt, that girl."

His mother had similar postcards from clients who went to Key West or the Carolinas to fish, men who came back brown and lean, in need of a shave. They laughed at the tanning bed and told her about Jimmy Buffet's bar. The waitresses there wore tight tank tops, they said. Even in January.

"I'd look better in eighty degrees too," she said.

Think about the sun, Pippin! Karla had written. A picture of El Morro, an old, sea-bashed fort.

Pete kept the postcard hidden.

"Who's it supposed to be?" asked Molly of his newest painting. They were crammed around the Formica table in the kitchen when she asked. In the basement he'd painted the shoulders and back of a slim, faceless girl in a tank top.

"Karla," said Pete without thinking. He watched as Emmett ate soggy Cheerios from a bright yellow bowl with his fingers. He wanted to speak again before she did. "I've only been as far as New York." He looked out at the cove and the pines.

Then Molly spoke. "That was with me, Pete. I went to New York City with you."

Emmett flung his bowl to the floor and neither of them budged to mop it up. And then the evening continued as usual, without any more confessions.

Pete feels his head bob and hears the waitress' voice say, "Refill," in a way that isn't a question. A man at the counter asks for a tuna melt.

He imagines holding on to the waitress' wide hips, burrowing in as she taps the pen on her pad.

He watches the water turn steely around the Old Orchard Beach pier, the last light slipping.

He remembers the descriptions of aquamarine sea in the *Savage* book Molly gave him. He tries to remember the reasons for that color in hot places—algae, reflection, refraction?

A foghorn belches from somewhere far away, and he sees that it's well past four. He finishes his cold tea. He smokes the last of the joint in a bathroom stall. He begins to make up a reasonable lie.

The tanks at the pound needed replacement valves. Grover's ran out.

They sent you to Old Orchard, without a hardware store in sight?

I needed to see Old Orchard. I needed to remember the Pirate Ship.

Why?

The truth? I needed to see if I could do it. Leave you. It's awfully tiring, the same thoughts. The same colors and tides.

On the pier the ice cream stand is boarded with plywood. The wind flaps at a bright blue tarp. The gulls should be there—ugly, beaky, squawking for scraps. But they aren't. He wants to be at the Thistle, where the bar is an old dory turned upside down, slick with shellac. There he can lean his elbows on the underside of the bow and feel the smooth cedar holding him up. He can have Belhaven on tap, the foam creamy.

The bartender, Jim, three years behind Pete in school, had once sneaked him a small glass of absinthe. "This shit will kill you," Jim said, knocking back a small measure himself.

Would it? Pete saw the most remarkable colors through the windshield—and then he'd puked in the woods, pulling over just in time.

It hadn't killed him.

Could he? Like Harold in *Harold and Maude*, always trying to end it.

He'd told Molly once, in high school, about wanting to drive right in, disobeying the curves, just letting the truck go straight. How tempting it would be, how right to ignore the arbitrary line of the road.

But he wouldn't do that, not for real. He was not Harold, and she was not Maude.

No. As a boy, at Popham, he'd gone climbing without shoes and cut the pads of his feet on dried barnacles. They sliced right through and the sting came quickly, mixed with salt, and he ran back to the blanket for his mother to fix it. How horrified he'd been, part of him leaking onto her towel like that.

Even someone else's bandaged arm or leg, wrapped up and mummified. It made him feel—he didn't know. It made him want to sit down. And the *Tribune* loved that shit, the *Little House on the Prairie* accidents. Missteps with axes and shipyard implements. Smash-ups on Route 27. The time Byler Sr. came into the pound with a fishhook in his arm. The time the old Ebbtide chef cut off his finger with a planer. Came to work on Monday as usual, hand wrapped up, head full of Vicodin. "Oh well," the chef said. He made a joke about being all thumbs and started slicing with his good hand propped against his waist, the wrapped-up stub a little brown at the tip.

Pete looks down at his hands. How good they've been to him so far.

Then he finds a pay phone and blurts out the valve lie to his wife.

At home the kitchen counter is clean. The beds have been made. There is no note.

The whale inside is still. *She took my child.*

But they'd only gone to the Y for family-swim. A guilty swish in his belly when the front door cracks open. Molly's eyes are a chlorinated pink, and Emmett's head is just beginning to dry.

It was me. I left her, he knows, and pats them both awkwardly on the shoulders.

8

AFTER WORK, INSTEAD OF bolting for Old Orchard again, Pete makes for the upside-down dory. He pushes open the Thistle door to see Flip Johnson, just as Flip Johnson turns to scowl at the dick who let in so much cold.

"Frenchie! No shit."

"Hey," says Pete.

"'*Highway run...*'"

Jim the bartender is too far away to interrupt. "Thought you were in the desert."

"Done with that shit," says Flip. His hair has grown out, a small lump of gray by his ear. "Working for Duggan this summer."

"Nice," says Pete. Duggan, who comes into the pound without taking off his foul-weather gear, fish guts on his boots.

"Still got the jacket," says Flip. He slaps at the bar and laughs at this. "You still painting?"

"Jackets?"

"Ha! More than jackets, should be."

A silence settles in, not a comfortable one. On TV the Packers and the Jets run around. Flip watches for a while and then groans as though he's been knocked in the groin himself.

"Hey—thanks for the beer," Pete says.

"Got time for another?"

"Have to run. Molly and all."

"Something I said?" He cracks a smile, his teeth still very white.

"Good to see you back."

"From the front, old top. Say hi to your girlie."

"Will do." *Get to the door.*

"Saw her at the bank. Quite the stunner, still."

At home, Molly watches David Lettermen talk to Pamela Andersen's tits. "Bar smell," says Molly. "Nice."

"Flip bought me one." He watches her.

She yawns. "Flip—yeah, saw him at the bank."

"He's here for the summer, apparently. Working for Duggan."

She laughs at something Dave says, doesn't look up.

"Unless he decides to re-enlist," says Pete. "Said you were a stunner, still."

"Might be safer than working for Duggan."

He drops it. She looked pleased by that, the stunner part. He opens a bottle of Beck's from the fridge and goes outside for a smoke, where the stars are still against the black. He stares, letting his heart speed for a while.

9

THEY TAKE THE BOAT TO MONHEGAN ISLAND on a bright, startling day in July and try to forget. Molly's parents pay for the hotel. Emmett will go to Story Land to ride his favorite, The Old Woman Who Lived in a Shoe, as many times as he wants.

"What makes this island different from any other island?" Molly says. She huddles in a cherry windbreaker, one she calls too touristy for town—thick with lining, shiny from lack of wear. She's on her second Shipyard from the tiny aft bar, and she looks sturdy to Pete in the sun. No make up, hair blowing wild. Someone who won't ever slip over the side.

The couple on the bench behind them read aloud in New Jersey voices: the Norse carvings, the remnants of the hermit's shack on Manana, which is the island that buffers Monhegan from rough seas. Boats can dock without smashing against the rocks.

"Useful, that," says Molly.

"The luck of geology," Pete says, feeling quite sober, feeling not in the mood for this game she has in mind.

The Coast Guard station is gone, the voices say. Nothing left on Manana but an old winding ridge where supplies had been hoisted. The shack where the hermit lived still there, sinking into the rocks.

"Fuck the hermit," Molly says.

"Easy," says Pete.

There are artists out there, posers with little studios, at least a dozen small galleries. There are crafts on roadside stands and an actual pottery barn. There's a one-room schoolhouse where the librarian has to teach.

Pete thinks, *It isn't a place for an anniversary, Monhegan. It's a place for a lobster roll and a quick ride back.*

They unpack and wander, watching the painters with broad hats and wheelbarrows stocked with easels, snacks, umbrellas, paper towels. The artists push their gear to the beach and the lighthouse and the cliffs, lurking by pine trees, even the lousy ones, standing on the bluffs like seers.

"Bring your sketchbook?" says Molly.

"Nope," says Pete. He wants to see the hermit shack. He wants to find forgotten things—cups or bottles or books. A woman on Fish Beach rents a skiff by the hour and they still have time, he says. They could pay her and be across the harbor before dark.

But Molly talks him out of it. Too windy, she says, and her butt hurts from too much sitting. They go to the general store and buy more Shipyard and drink on the trails instead.

"Could you stay out here?" she says. She left the tourist jacket at the inn. Her sweatshirt is exactly the shade of the water, he thinks. Pewter, with thin, pink tubing around the sleeve. She hooks an arm through his.

"I don't think so," says Pete.

After dinner they walk to the shipwreck—a beached, rusted hull and other random pieces still litter the rocks. "That's what happens when you mess with the ocean," says Molly. Why should the islanders be the ones to haul the shit away, she says. Not their fault the ship landed poorly.

Pete clenches his flashlight. It's cold enough for a hat with the sun down, which Molly wears and Pete does not. He stops and faces her on the path, shining his light at her feet. He swipes her hat and balls it in his fist.

"Hey," she says. "It's cold."

He pulls off her sweatshirt and paws at her breasts and quickly, quickly, they do it right behind the life-ring post, the ocean roaring, the lighthouse beam far away.

In the morning they hike out the booze and sit on a stone bench just beginning to warm in the sun. Pete squints at the gingerbread houses, window trim in matching white and worn gray swaths of shingle in between. Houses made of driftwood, looks like. He starts to tell Molly but she gets up—her butt hurts again.

They look at clippings in the Island Museum between beams of floating dust and Molly finds a drawing of the hermit, his beard shaggy, his eyes sad.

"He left Galway in a leaky skiff," she says. "Just said fuck it and went to sea."

It happens.

"He ran into Manana. Didn't plan to," she reads. "Raised the goats for milk."

In a back room, "The Art of Monhegan" crams the walls. Dead artists and living artists thrown together. "Study for *The Invocation*," Molly says. "Circa 1903, artist unknown."

"Whoever he was, it's a pretty shitty copy," says Pete. *You don't have to read everything out loud.* He remembers the original from *Jansen's*, the square-hipped Tahitian girl reaching up for something high. Like the curvy waitress at Old Orchard Beach.

They skip the library. But in the graveyard they walk between the slanted names, and Molly traces the faded letters with her thumb. He'll sketch this at home, his wife at the worn stones. The bright grass underneath her old boots, poking through.

10

FOR A WHILE, AFTER Monhegan, they drink tea again and Pete is safe with Molly on the bedspread, with the mugs they try hard not to spill, which they do spill, a sudden jerk of a limb and a wetness that creeps. "It washes out," said Molly, but it doesn't, not completely. There will be odd brown mudflats that merge with the blue. His mug is red and hers is green, on sale from the potter's place on Monhegan, lopsided from the too-hot kiln.

It's risky to touch her again. That's how the Ebbtide breakfasts started. A way to get away from the mugs and Molly's too-warm body.

Instead Pete goes to the basement and tries to remember the way the sun slid across the cliffs on Monhegan. There was something about the light there. It's hard for Pete to stop thinking about it, though he can't quite recall the shades in that windowless place, with the washer and dryer and fungus on the walls. She's right—he should have a proper space with natural light. But not the girlie shed where she'd written *Flip Johnson*. He can build himself a new hut in the sun, away from the dryer and the mold. He can buy an easel and go to the Point with a goddamn wheelbarrow.

He imagines the Byler brothers, stopping to share a blunt before facing their own sad wives at home. *"Saw you at the Point, Pecker.*

Working hard or hardly working?"

He thinks himself back to the basement and by noon the colors are almost right. This is more comforting than the tea, like a hum in his throat, a busy motor. He's done it—turned the grip into something recognizable. Shades and lines and shapes.

Until Molly belts, *Going to family swim. Still alive down there?* She taps the basement door with her boot as she leaves.

The words form themselves easily inside. *Yes, still alive.*

He tries to remember other shades—the surly blue-black of the bugs still living in tanks, claws and tails piled.

He waits for Molly and Emmett to be gone, for the house to take on the lovely, quiet buzz of just him. Crunch of gravel fading on the too-long road.

That night, he knew, he'd park in the black, slick lot of the Thistle again.

When he sees Karla, elbows propped on the overturned dory, his first thought is, *I'm so much better at French kissing now.* She's leaning in, inches from Jim the bartender's beard, her hair cut short, her face thinner. Jim stands up and says Pete's name, just like the TV bartender, and, like TV, all the Thursday-night drinkers turn to see Pete there in his red knitted cap, knitted by Molly.

Karla does a little shriek and whirls herself toward him.

He feels his cheeks crack, feels the skin stretch there without effort.

"Goddamn," she says. Her breath is hot. She wears a shrunken turtleneck and, below a slice of brown belly, a buckle with rhinestones. Her leather boots look real. Black with red tips, an oval slash on each pointed toe.

"I'm a proper shit-kicker now," she says, watching his eyes. She rattles her glass, and Jim pours more Malibu. Her straw is smudged with coral pink. "Saw your mum," she says.

Yes, thinks Pete. Got her eyebrows waxed. And no roots showing through. His mother hadn't been able to remember Pete's cell number, offhand. Told her that Molly and Emmett were well.

"Hates me, that old cow."

He wonders why she's speaking this way, like a lobsterman. "You done with the ship?" Pete starts. It's hard not to look at her belt. She must be cold in that half-shirt; he wants to give her his hat.

Jim listens and pretends not to. He pours a Belhaven, mops the dripping foam from the bar. The coaster is new, and Pete watches a circle bleed into the white.

"I'm on leave," Karla says. Her eyelids seem heavy. "It's awesome to see you." She pushes her straw around with her finger and studies his jaw.

It is pretty awesome.

She asks about the pound and his paintings, says she likes the one on the wall of the beauty shop, the row of Townsend Avenue stores.

"Did that ages ago," he says.

"You didn't put Nesta's in there. Remember?" Funky place, crammed with albums. Nesta wore shawls, lots of makeup. The store smelled like dead flowers.

Yes. He remembers. Overpriced because there was nowhere else to go, before Bull Moose Music and Vinyl Haven.

She spent her allowance on 45s, she says. "Do They Know It's Christmas" and "One Night in Bangkok" and "Purple Rain" and "Gloria"—Laura Branigan, remember her?

"Sure," says Pete.

There was something about owning the song yourself, she says, the freedom to play it whenever. And that weird yellow nipple you needed. Without it you were screwed, your records useless.

Nipple. He'd forgotten what it's like to hear her talk, the raspiness that made her seem older in the school plays.

"Anyway," she says, remembering her point, "what are you painting now?"

He tells her what he can, then finds himself talking about Old Orchard, the lie of it. How different he'd felt driving there, if only for a day.

She nods. She orders more drinks. Jim nods. She doesn't ask questions that require Pete to say "Molly" or "Emmett." Then she shows him pictures of Malta and Papeete on her phone, shots of her in the same pink bikini, a pink so light it looks like she's naked. Sprawled on the sand by water that looks very far away. He wonders who took the pictures.

"You have to go there," she says. "The beaches are wicked." There are lots of jobs on the ship: Pho-tog, Croupier, Sommelier. "They're usually Filipino, but they don't have to be."

"Actually, I'm half Filipino," he says. He can be funny.

And then they're in his Subaru on the way to the Point and he's thinking, *Someone will notice her car at the Thistle all night* and already he's constructed the non-lie: *She was drunk, I drove her home.* He spots Emmett's *Elmo* book and slides it underneath the seat.

At the Point he stops the engine and reclines, feels the heat in the car begin to fade. Feels her mouth on his neck and his throat and his stomach. Lets her stay there and stay there, cupping her breasts that feel bigger, moaning as the lighthouse beam swoops just over the hood.

"Missed your peter, Peter," she says, her voice rough, her hair soft. On her left hand is the tiny diamond ring he'd noticed hours ago. He turns up the radio and kisses her on the mouth.

Later, with Molly a warm, quiet pile beside him, his head still thick, he thinks, *I could do that. Take pictures on the pool deck for Pirate Night.* Karla said they went around the dining room with eye patches and stuffed parrots. "And they buy that shit, the passengers," she'd said. Ten, fifteen dollars a picture, and the Pho-togs make commission.

They'd sneak into a life vest closet, a dressing room. He'd sweep back the glittery costumes and they'd be buried, the wall bracing them.

He thinks about the other Ents. girls she'd described, the ones who couldn't sing and had to wear sarongs slung low on their hips for Tropical Night. (The trick, Karla said, was to make it look like the material could slide off easily, even though it couldn't.) The bartenders would give them free drinks, grateful for their bare stomachs and bikini tops, their armfuls of plastic leis.

On a ship, his eyes would shine like Karla's.

11

NEXT TIME KARLA TELLS him about the absinthe bar in Papeete.

"Gauguin was addicted to absinthe," Pete says, remembering.

"It's all about Gauguin there," she says. "Didn't his dick fall off or something?"

"He had syphilis," says Pete.

"Those nasty, nasty French." She frees herself from the seatbelt, unzipping his jeans again.

When her parents are gone, they go to her cottage, where there are more photos, stacks of albums with sand dollars and seashells on the covers, enough to fill the bottom shelf of the entertainment unit Pete recognized from the Pier One catalog, one Molly had earmarked.

Karla describes how she felt in each photo—she knows she looked happy, but she wasn't happy.

She'd been depressed, she says. Clinically.

Clinically. Pete thinks of Bunsen burners and steel countertops in Chemistry class. "Maybe you should be on Prozac," he says.

"I am on Prozac."

He waits for her to crack into her *Chorus Line* face but she doesn't.

He wonders how much longer before Brett at the pound calls his cell. *Fucking long lunch break,* he'd said the day before.

"It took a lot to figure it out," she says. "AA meetings. CODA." She's combing her hairdo with her fingers, stopping to delicately break away knots. Fine, blonde strands get caught on her ring.

Pete doesn't ask but she tells him anyway.

"Codependents Anonymous. I went in New York. What a drag I was, in places like Barbados and Tortola. Tortola! And so much booze—every night, wasted. I think it changed me, actually changed the organization of my brain."

You still drink like a fish, Pete thinks. "You still drink," he says. He nudges her hip to make it nicer.

"Not as much," she says. "Shouldn't you be at home with your boy now?"

She doesn't say Molly's name, so he pulls her back down. She slides a bright red bible from the entertainment unit and reads to him from Corinthians and they curl up together like a comma on the Pier One rug.

At home he ignores Molly's face. He thinks of Flip. *She had her fling.*

But it doesn't help. His insides feel very large and very small at the same time.

Karla tells him more about the ship—how gleaming and enormous it looks. How she'd wanted to run from it at first. It isn't real, just a giant tooth berthed in Palma. She knows the right words at least: berth, port, starboard. Not a boat but a *ship.*

She got seasick! It made her want to swipe at things, like a constant bug buzzing too close. Her stomach felt empty and loose even when it was full. Her mouth watered. All those Windjammer and Whaler rides in the harbor. The Reggae Cruise! She hadn't expected it, not being seaworthy. She'd never needed the dumb wristbands, the ear patches.

But in her bunk she felt the walls around her shifting—a creak that probably meant a stairwell was splitting. The shampoo bottle in the shower fell and cracked open and leaked its green goo down the drain. The porthole blinked with black then blue. She wished for something to hurl itself against her portion of glass—something living. A starfish, an eel. (*Were they far enough down for that?* Pete wonders.) Some nights the Promenade Deck doors were locked and the Captain asked Security to guard the doors, just in case drunken yahoos decided to barge through on a dare. In the crew mess, during an Atlantic crossing, a plate slid from the table and crashed. Karla just sat and watched it—they all did, without laughing.

The ship had stabilizers, the Safety Officer reminded them. Which made sinking impossible.

The way she did his voice made Pete think of William Shatner. He wants to picture someone much uglier.

In the Caribbean she got her sea legs. She drank more. She went to the crew deck when no one was there, when the night and the daytime seemed at opposite ends and there was just black in between (3:00 AM was good for this), when there were sounds and not people: the cruise control of the engine thrumming, the water slushing beneath, a giant jet skier kind of splash—cheerful, vigorous—and the weary churning of the engine underneath, working hard. She wasn't supposed to be there past eleven, which was another reason why she liked to go. She listened from a greasy sun lounger, plastic slats flapping where her neck should lean. She drank the gin and tonic she'd brought up from the crew bar, then ate the ice.

She felt like a famous person sometimes, smoking on the beach in Grenada with her cabin mate, Samantha. They bought new sarongs from a market stall—bright orange, bright yellow, a giant salamander, batiked. But you'd never know it was a salamander unless you spread on the floor or the sand.

Sam borrowed the Casino Manager's key and used his single, empty cabin for the night with a passenger from Sweden. But a cleaner caught them in the morning, high and fucking, and then Sam had to leave the ship for good. The Casino Manager got to stay.

"She was dumb to get caught," says Pete. The heat blasts. He smears a circle on the foggy car window and watches the black waves outside.

Then Karla decided she needed to be healthier. She bought new sneakers in St. Maarten but trying to run on deck was impossible, she said, even when it was calm. The spray made everything slippery.

She looks at her ring. "I have to stop acting like all my adventures are behind me."

Maybe they are behind you, Pete thinks. *Stop talking, for fuck's sake.*

At midnight he drives her home, lies to Molly, goes to bed. He wishes for the whale, which would be familiar.

He dreams he's painting the vast white hull—strapped in, making strokes until it's clean.

In the morning Molly reaches for him and he holds her too tight. "Mmm," she says. "*Squeeze*. Stop it, squeezer." But he doesn't. He holds her until his arm goes numb.

12

PETE BEGINS TO RECOUNT his own adventures to Karla. It's his turn.

1) The penguin he saw once, squatting on a rock at the Point. (He deletes Molly from the scene.) It turned its head and then didn't budge for an hour, its white chest facing the road, its black back to the waves. It was a frigid day and Pete pictured the thing on an ice floe, cruising away from home.

It would be his totem, he decided. Like the cave bear for Daryl Hannah in that movie.

He'd thought Molly would find this nice, the idea of a life-bird. "Maybe you should work at the new age store," she'd said.

He'd looked it up later in a bird book at the library and saw that it was not a penguin, but something called an auk. Whatever it was, it didn't belong there.

"That's nice," says Karla. "A life bird. Mine would have to be a turtle."

"As a life bird?"

"No, you said totem. Because it carries its house on its back. Or an ermine, maybe." She doesn't explain.

2) His bachelor night in Portland, which Campbell had arranged—the shots and the steaks, the bad karaoke bar and the lazy stripper. Campbell collapsed in the men's room. Then he shoved an envelope at Pete, filled with twenties, and got himself in a cab.

The sign outside the club had a neon rooster: *Cock.*

Pete wasn't exactly shocked by the place, his head loose with booze already, but he was startled into an unfamiliar discomfort, and the discomfort made him wonder about himself. He paid ten dollars and, without looking, the large woman stamped Pete's wrist exactly where a razor might slice. The stamp said *WHORE.*

"Wait, what?" he said to the doorwoman but she pretended not to hear.

And then he saw the men, actually dancing on the bar. Naked, almost—their bikini bottoms pushed down to the very edge of their hips, just where the pubes began, hair pushed up above the elastic, balls mashed into a tiny balloon of cloth, bare asses seen clearly in the vast mirror behind the bar.

He stopped. Someone said, "Careful, guy."

Pete had all sorts of questions: Did they shower before or after work or both? Were they high? What had the want ad requested?

He remembered he had WHORE stamped on his wrist.

The bartender was also wearing bikini briefs, a more sanitary version, no pubes on view. "A Heineken," said Pete, but he said it too quietly and had to shout.

With his beer in hand, Pete stood as far from the naked dancers as possible.

There was kissing and groping already, men with men and women with women and women with men. Pete was jostled, like Karla on the streets of Shanghai. He drank his beer. He remembered an article about the kinds of drinks people ordered and what this revealed about them. That beer meant—and wine meant—and mixed drinks meant—

And then there was a band playing Prince songs. The bass player looked like Prince, but taller. The keyboardist had fake breasts and very broad shoulders.

Pete had another Heineken and then another, able to look more closely at the men dancing on the bar. He had two Important Thoughts in quick succession and lost them.

He wondered what was happening in the long bathroom line.

And then the Prince band whooshed itself off and a man in a leather thong unfolded a massage table. Pete stood by the stage and heard someone ask if that was his jacket. The masseuse was asking him, didn't want lotion to get on it. He winked when he said "lotion."

No, no, Pete said, *not mine*—he mimed this, shouting above the remix of a Blondie song he knew but couldn't name.

What about the drums? the masseuse mimed back. *Yours?*

Not mine, Pete said. He tried a smile. *I look like I'm a drummer?*

And then one of the bar dancers came out and slipped off his thong. Had this been in the want ad too? And was the man completely naked? Yes, he certainly appeared to be. He covered his stuff with his hands and flopped onto his stomach and the masseuse squirted lotion from a large pump bottle. (Like the peach yogurt Pete liked to eat for lunch at the pound sometimes, in the back.)

And the lotion was everywhere on the man's very tan legs and butt. His arms fell limp on either side of the table.

That would feel nice, Pete thought, to have the legs rubbed after standing so much.

But was the man actually able to enjoy it? And what was about to happen on that stage, when the man was completely unknotted and moisturized?

The drummer arrived, annoyed. He needed to get his equipment off stage—he hadn't been informed. He ignored the masseuse and steered it all off fast.

And then Pete left, before he could see what the two men would do next.

He wanted to call Molly, describe what he'd seen.

But she'd put down the phone and wonder.

He'd paint them, the near-naked men. He'd try to make sense of it, maybe while he was naked himself.

At the hotel, Campbell was slumped in the bathtub, fully clothed. Pete turned off the light and closed the bathroom door.

"On the ship I kissed a girl from Russia once," says Karla, when he pauses to relight the joint.

"Yeah?" he says. *Shut up. It's my story.*

Number three, which Pete doesn't describe to Karla, is his wedding at the Wilson Memorial Chapel, which normally had to be reserved a year in advance. But Molly's parents knew the pastor, who bumped a couple from Connecticut to chilly late September.

Pete had three glasses of champagne in the back of Campbell's car and Molly said later she'd been able to smell it, facing him in the small stone church. He'd nicked his chin with his razor, and a tiny brown dot of dried blood clung there. He'd shaved his goatee, as per Molly's request.

When he slid the ring on, he thought, *This is a capable hand.* It was manicured with pretty lavender tips, courtesy of Cutting Edge. He thought about where the hand had been. She still called her hair strawberry, even though it wasn't. Her eyes were the same pretty brown. Amber or hazelnut.

That's a flavor, not a color. Could it be a color? Not really—hazelnut is like Nutella.

Which he'd tasted only once, at a New Year's party thrown by Molly's bank boss, who'd just returned from Switzerland. Pete had been the only one wearing a chamois shirt.

"It's just Nutella. You can get it at Shop N Save," another teller said, slabbing a Wheat Thin.

But you couldn't. You had to go to Portland.

Then someone at the bank party told a joke about being sent to the Italian section of Shop N Save when he asked for taco shells.

"There's an Italian section?" someone else said.

All of this came to Pete rapid-fire in the dark church at the Point on his wedding day. Molly's skin felt unusually cool. Outside, he knew, the sea would be shining.

And outside, stepping into the sun together as married people, a red Saab with Illinois plates slowed and a blonde girl took their picture from the rolled-down back window.

"Mazel tov!" she shouted.

Campbell made another toast on the rocks, and the Byler brothers honked from the lobster boat they'd anchored. They hadn't been invited.

And then they all cruised around the harbor in a party boat. Just like the Reggae Cruise, Pete thought. Except there was no "No Woman, No Cry."

13

"I HAVE TO GO BACK to New York," says Karla at Ocean Point. They're parked near the chapel again.

"You should," Pete says. His chest heaves. *What about my Pho-tog job?*

"I'm trying to figure out when." She makes her pretty lips pull around a Camel Light. She taps at the chicken pox scar on her forehead to indicate the *figure out* part—her brain.

"Don't," he says.

"I have to."

"I mean, don't smoke," Pete lies. "If you want to be a singer."

"It helps, I think." She drops the cigarette out the window and falls onto him then, her full weight on his chest. "Makes me sound worldly."

He hopes she'll stay that way, leaning into him. He doesn't move. He can contain her weight, most of it, in the space of his lap and his chest.

"When I don't smoke, I get headaches."

He feels her jaw move against his shoulder. *That's because you're too skinny. Too amped on nicotine, coffee—everything too much.* She'd been like that in high school too.

"There's a picture of me," she says.

"I must have seen it then."

But he hadn't seen it: Karla in a restaurant with an ex and the ex's college friends and they were all wicked happy and high and she was trying hard but in the picture she looks like she doesn't want to be there, not one bit. It's embarrassing after the fact, how unhappy she looked when everyone else looked so frigging happy.

"But you said they were high," says Pete.

"Yeah, but beyond that—you could see they really meant it."

The ex got up early to go to work as a brunch waiter and she stayed in the cold apartment alone, waiting for her leave to be over so she could go back to the ship and sing again and sunbathe and sleep in the Safety Officer's suite on the bridge.

"I had flashes in my eyes," she says. "Like stigmata. Stigmata?"

"Astigmatism?"

"No, like Christ. Like it was a sign." Because she'd told the Safety Officer she was staying with a girlfriend in London when really she was staying with the ex-boyfriend in Dover.

The point being, she went blind in one eye. It wouldn't go away. She prayed that it would go but it wouldn't. She opened her eyes first thing and tried to convince herself that it was morning blurriness, just her eyes adjusting. But she could see a squiggle drifting down, over and over, a squiggle that expanded and blocked out light and then she couldn't see out of the eye, not at all. She couldn't read or cut things with a knife. She couldn't drive—not that she would on the wrong side of the road. She had to look at things off center to see things clearly.

They even went to visit the ex's parents, who took her to an ophthalmologist who said she was fine. Had she been using a computer a lot? Reading in bad light?

No, said Karla.

Eye strain, the eye doctor said. It would go away.

And it did go away—

So why this long story? Pete wonders.

—once she stopped feeling guilty about cheating on the Safety Officer. Who'd been cheating on his wife all along.

Pete's stomach aches. He opens his window. He asks her if she wants to smoke from the bong and she says yes but the story apparently still isn't over.

From the ship Karla wrote a thoughtful letter to the ex in Dover, who sent her things back to Bay Harbor in a duffel. There was no note in the duffel.

Why hadn't he put in a note? She still wonders about that.

"Because you left him," Pete says. He lights the bong. What's wrong with her?

"No, I didn't. I went back to work."

"What did your letter say, then?"

But she snatches the lighter and doesn't tell him anything else about it.

The cold waves are gray, despite the sun. Pete wants to be sleeping.

But she talks about the porthole in her cabin again, the lid bolted shut, the total darkness until she borrowed the pliers and cracked the cover and let the light in a little. It wasn't safe to do that, the Safety Officer said, and it wasn't even real light; it was water. Water diffused by light. Couldn't that harm a person, change her over time? Having to adjust to darkness in this way? Maybe her brain got blurry with the effort.

Pete doesn't know what to say about this.

"Like alcohol," she says. "Like I was saying before. It can change the brain over time."

"You should stick to weed."

The thing about drinking is that it's never as much fun as it seems it will be, she says. She keeps thinking it will make things larger than they really are, more interesting. But instead it just makes her fuzzy.

Like drinking at the Thistle, Pete thinks. *With me.*

"But when it's right there in front of me, I can't *not* have it."

He drives her home. He goes back to the pound. If he ever works on a ship, he decides, sun too bright on the empty town landing, he won't get distracted by portholes.

At home, Pete farts a lot. Molly thinks it's the beer. Emmett finds the empties piled up in the kitchen, and Molly has to snatch them away. Bottle caps like roaches on the floor by the pail.

"You seem chipper lately," says Molly.

"I shouldn't be?"

"You should be. You aren't usually." But her tone is easy. Her sweatshirt is ripped at the shoulder. She's making oatmeal for Emmett, who's decided he likes foods with raisins best.

She yawns, stirs.

"You're lovely," he says. He tries to remember Campbell's book.

"Sure," she says, her dimples showing, making it true.

Later, he feels nothing but a jangle of wanting to get back to Karla talking a blue streak.

In his basement, he smokes and takes the pills he's been saving and studies the books Molly gave him. He paints.

As the weather turns, as Karla puts off New York, it's easy enough to take her to Oven's Mouth, where the trees are full and the paths are quiet. It's easy to undress her behind the bush Pete crouched behind as a boy. She has pine needle imprints on her back and he peels them off and laughs and they take the pills together and do it again.

He thinks, *She's been to lots of islands.* He grabs hold of her arms too tightly, and she asks him not to. "*Vahine*," he whispers. He traces the fading tan line just above her nipple. "*Tehura*."

"What did you say?" she says.

"Nothing." *A woman of Polynesian descent.*

"You should shave—it's getting prickly." She slides her tongue along his cheek.

He closes his eyes and feels the sand on his feet.

"Are you growing a beard?"

He doesn't answer. *Sand in his brushes, making grainy patterns on the canvas.*

"Do you want me to do it like this?" she says.

Yes, he says. He doesn't say please.

In the town library, Pete twirls the globe, streaking his finger across the Pacific, a faded dark blue. Not midnight blue, but close. He touches Tahiti.

The island smells like nutmeg, he decides. He could watch the ship sail away, simply refusing to go back to the gangway.

Would they come back to retrieve him, once they knew? Would someone tell the Safety Officer? Would it be worth it for just one man?

In the basement, the art books help Pete see:

The beach is vast, the ukulele is battered. The painter left it out too long and the strings are warped, salted. When he plucks the lowest sting, it cries in a bended way, a note curving down like a tone in Mandarin.

His ukulele can speak Mandarin and he can not!

He wears a sarong, a bright orange one, a color he then creates on his palette and smears on one corner of his new canvas, one of five he'll send back to Paris. Then he'll sail even further, to the Marquesas.

Next Pete remembers the barnacles, cutting his feet long ago.

Then another time, walking barefoot on the sand with his mother, having to watch out for beached jellyfish at Old Orchard. He sees a pretty shell and steps in the living goop and the pain spreads like a color inside, pink to red very fast. His mother has to squeeze his foot hard to make it go away, ooze the sting back out like a sponge.

There's still a little nub on his big toe where the center of the pain had came from, a bit of tentacle absorbed and locked. He presses it now, gazes at the washer and dryer and his shitty canvases. Sea life inside him still.

The pain keeps him up nights, so he takes more pills.

Some days it isn't any color at all. Just a slice of something he shouldn't have swallowed. Pain like a jellyfish sting.

But when the Tahitian girl arrives, the pain goes away. She slips into his bed and begins to stroke at him, hard.

He wants to tell Molly, invite her along—she'll find it funny.

I'll have to build a hut of my own, he realizes, and drifts off to sleep at last.

In the morning he tells Molly about the hut, hoping she'll say something smirky like, *You'll need a permit for that.* He feels pleasantly dizzy still. He'll answer, *A permit from Officer Dicky? Fuck that!*

But instead she sets the kettle down, turns to look at him square. "There are pills you can take, you know. Other kinds. Pills that can make you less sad." There's a pleading look he hasn't seen before.

He doesn't want to be less sad. He wants to be less awake at night. It's tiring to see colors all day. Tiring in the mind but not tiring enough in his body.

With other pills, he wouldn't see the colors anymore. The sting would be cured for good.

She turns around and doesn't look up from the stove. She won't ask again.

14

AT THE THISTLE, TWO hours pass, and still Karla doesn't show.

He drives by the cottage, her high basement window still dark. He calls from the Thistle again until her father answers.

He leaves, forgetting to tip Jim.

Two weeks later, at Cutting Edge, his mother slips a postcard across the counter, facedown. Her lips are taut. Champagne pink. A very famous building under her French Tips.

Hi, Karla has written on the other side, with a tiny heart above the i.

*

There's no camping, officially, but Pete thinks he might camp. He'll stuff the pup tent and the poles in his duffel with his easel. He knows a place, beyond the shipwreck but before Burnt Head, where the pines would hide the shape of it for a while, where the day-trippers wouldn't think to look, where the locals wouldn't care either, too many prickers surrounding. And what if they did? He'd explain succinctly, he'd use the words stored up.

I am the bastard son of Paul Gauguin.

They'll laugh. They'll call him Frenchie or faggot and the burliest ones from the VFD will tell him to take his tent down, a-sap.

"Make me," he'll say.

They'll make him. They'll get him a room at the Oar House or the Island Inn or tell him to fix up the hermit's shack himself. He'll sell paintings to tourists. Slap on eggshell white and touch up porches. He'll get some chickens, perhaps some goats.

The point being, he'll be allowed to stay.

And little Emmett will hear stories about his father the Famous Painter, who lived out his last days as a savage, *able to work, love and die*. A stone in the island cemetery with his family name. A place for Emmett to mourn and wonder. And Molly, if she wants. She can trace her pretty finger along the indent that is his name, her sweatshirt zipped up to the top, green shoots coming up at her feet.

Come spring, his wife will have the driveway pocks filled up with expensive dirt her cousins will spill and even. It will wash away and the ice will return and again she'll pay to make it smoother.

He knows she'll have to explain it to them eventually, the rugged, sober people she's related to. But maybe she'll also feel relieved. She'll look out at her son smashing ice in his Bean boots and the line of the chilly harbor through the trees. She won't miss the churning feelings, the years of basement rumblings, the breaking and drifting in her very own home.

She'll say, if asked, that her husband took too much Oxy, enough to make his brain not quite right for good. Privately, she'll suppose there is a certain charge in it, a spark in being untethered all the time. In drifting to places too hard to map.

*

Molly watches her son, who seems to like the holes the way they are. Maybe he remembers crunching ice pockets in his snowsuit, his skinny father just up ahead, the way he was silly outside, googly-eyed and coughing—breaking the solid panes with high jumps, sending ice splinters up. The way he'd smoked in a careful way, tucking the spent butt in his pocket instead of flicking it into the snow. Inside, maybe it's harder to remember his father clearly. They hadn't been in the same rooms together much.

Molly brings Emmett to Ebbtide for cocoa and doesn't have to tell the waitress, whose name is Betty Thompson, grandmother of a boy in Emmett's grade, that she wants a table for two. She nods to the Byler brothers, who take off their ski caps when she comes in. She leaves an extra dollar for Handsome Flip, back making eggs, because she knows the tips are pooled and because he doubles their order of French toast and bacon. Eight pieces, lean strips, the powdered sugar pretty in the neat syrup pool. Scrawled notes on napkins just for her. She hears him humming from the kitchen—the chorus of a song she liked a long time ago.

Karla

New York City, 2003

THE CRUISE SHIP SAILS and Karla does not. She still has a tan from Papeete. She lives on her own in Hell's Kitchen. She figures she can sublet when she goes to sea again, when Head Office in Florida calls her back to be an Entertainer. She tells everyone back in Maine she's just on leave. Temporary. She keeps thinking about Bay Harbor. Whether to go back there, though she hasn't been back since high school.

For now she hears the happy hour voices floating up from the bar below as she stirs Paul Newman sauce, a few fresh vegetables to beef it up, a trick her mother taught her during times when there was no beef. There are yips and shouts from the bar, people with office jobs pinching each other, letting the looseness of alcohol make them sound like teenagers. They unbutton the top notch of their shirts and blouses, she imagines. The shouting makes her lonely, like a keg party in the woods she can't find. The few times she ordered wine alone in a bar in Manhattan it was too dim to read. She didn't know what to do with her hands except lift the glass up and down. The bartender took pity and asked where she was from, what she did for a living, what she was doing later.

In her recurring dream, Karla is in a high school musical. *Les Miserables,* maybe. Something with wigs and corsets. She forgets the words (though it's remarkable how many words she *does* remember, all these years later, and a piece of her dreaming brain recognizes this. *Good for you.*) Molly Townsend is onstage too, in a frilly dress she's squeezed herself into. Everyone sings and dances and doesn't hear as Karla says, leaning in, *Screw you.* Molly's open mouth is a perfect, pretty O of shock.

In the dream the dance captain turns to Karla and says, "You really are heartless, cruel. You're not just acting. You really are this way. Amazing." And as she says it, Karla believes it. The dance captain can see Karla's brain believing it.

But it's such a marvelous feeling, to say the true thing. Even if she's hated for saying it. *Screw you.*

Later on, the cast of *Les Mis* is on the waterfront working together, assembling boats and traps, and Karla can't do any of it right. She has no instinct for how and where things lock together. Molly loses her patience and leans in and says, *Useless.* She holds a heavy tool. It's an insult much worse than Karla's.

Then she wakes up.

Mornings, Karla opens the medicine cabinet and takes two pills: birth control and folic acid, the same color and size. "If you're ever going to have children," her mother once said, "you should take folic acid so they don't have birth defects. And don't tweeze your eyebrows. Once you start, it's very hard to stop."

But people have warped, defective children every day, Karla wants to say. They mess them up in all kinds of ways—it can't be helped.

After that Karla equates tweezing with defects. Something very bad will happen if she continues to tweeze, maybe a defect to herself, her own brow—cancer of the brow. Maybe plucking makes the empty hair sockets fill up with bad juices, which solidify and slowly turn to tumors. But on the ship the dance captain had insisted, in front of all the other well-tweezed dancers. *Brooke Shields?* she said to Karla.

Now Karla does it every morning, after her pills—it wakes her up, the little jabs of emptiness she makes. A way to focus and plan her day around auditions and temping before the itchy feeling in the stomach creeps in again, the feeling of being alone too long.

How do people live alone forever? Some people do. She isn't one of those people.

Karla likes the subway when it isn't too full—the jostle of it, the rhythm, the way she can get there from here. The strange people she doesn't have to talk to, standing close.

The outer boroughs are better connected, her father says. Couldn't she move to Queens? The Bronx?

The Bronx is not an option. Besides, Manhattan has several amazing new-fangled structures called bridges. It isn't like Bay Harbor, with parts of coast jutting out into the vast, choppy Atlantic.

On September 11th it was the bridges that kept everybody stuck there, he reminds her. And did she have her swine flu shot? Probably best to avoid the subways altogether.

I have hand sanitizer, she says. They hang up. She doesn't want to talk about that day in September anymore.

And then she worries about the bridges. Could she swim to Brooklyn or New Jersey if she had to? Could she walk to New Rochelle?

She keeps checking her cell phone for missed calls from Ft. Lauderdale, center of all things cruise.

She emails Rachel: *I miss Maine.* She gives notice at the temp office. She sublets for the summer to a law school student who doesn't blink when she bumps up the rent to $1500 a month. She takes a long, slow Chinatown bus to Boston, then a Trailways bus to Portland, where her mother, waiting in the Subaru, wants to hear everything right then and there.

Rachel gets a sitter so they can go out to McSeagull's and look at high school yearbooks. Lots of midnight toker Steve Miller references and *We're outta here*'s. Molly Townsend: Most Likely to Succeed.

"They should have given you one," Rachel says to Karla. They're drinking Bailey's, just like they used to. But now it's from little glasses, not the bottle. "A superlative."

"Best ass," says Karla. Rachel doesn't disagree.

The next weekend Rachel takes her to a party on Squirrel Island and someone, a summer boy, is talking about astrology and Karla is interested in this. It would be such a relief if the stars are in charge of it all. She may have said this to him out loud. The boy has floppy blond hair and the easy laugh of a rich person and so, for a change, Karla speaks without planning the words first. "I'm Cancer/Leo cusp," she explains, and instead of smirking at her eagerness to speak, the blond boy nods as though this makes perfect sense, as though she's just outlined a complicated proof he's been considering too.

"You look like a Leo, but you act like a Cancer," he says, providing the triangular dot *therefore*. He says other words, like *thoughtful*, *creative*, *moon child*.

How does he know? They've only just met.

She looks like she's supposed to be the life of the party, the boy explains, pulling others out of themselves.

Yes. But inside she's doing virtual yoga, bending down into the familiar and hollowed-out bones of herself. It's quieter there. She doesn't have to explain to anyone. The Cancer girl listens and wants to make a beautiful home. (*You'll make a beautiful home*, she's read many times in her horoscope.) She used to love her home, her own room at home in Maine, with the walls and corners she knew so well. The afghan and the mossy colors everywhere. Her own record player and her own box of 45s.

The Leo horoscope promises she will eventually succeed. *You are the LIFE OF THE PARTY.* It's a comfort to see it, the cruise ship girl peeking out from the little Cancer house.

The cute stranger leaves to get a beer and then there's talk around her about things she can't comment on, the yacht club and someone's graduation from Wellesley. She waits for the right gaps in the paragraphs to fall, tries to nudge her foot in a little, just before the closing sentence so she won't be interrupted herself. It's hard to time it exactly. She blurts, she has to, and it's at the wrong time, the wrong thing. She's missed something, a crucial thread. And then the door bangs shut and they're talking about something new.

She has to pay attention and catch up. She needs to say something soon because—smiling, smiling, looking like a Leo but acting like a Cancer. *Why isn't the pretty girl saying anything? Is she dumb? Damaged?*

How disappointing to be so transparent. Everyone already knows how fucked up she is.

"I work on a cruise ship," she says at last. She keeps talking once she starts—she doesn't know when she'll get her chance again. She has so much to say but nobody asks her. She hates them for not asking.

Then Rachel sails across the lawn and drives her home. It's just like high school again.

"The second date is always so much harder," Karla says, trying to explain it to Rachel in the car. Karla's words are very loud in her mind and the black, empty road is the same as it's always been. Where are the lights? It's spaceship-dark out there. "On the first date you use up your best stories," she says, trying to peel the

Tori Amos sticker from the glove compartment. "You wear your favorite dress." The trick is not to go on the second date at all.

"You'll sleep it off," Rachel says from somewhere far away.

They had a secret club, once. They made a plan to get out by boat. "It literally sucks the lifeblood from you," Rachel said then, "if you stay in this turd town too long."

She said it a lot, and Karla believed her. "How long is too long? Twenty-five years?"

"Eighteen."

Their relatives had missed the cut off. It was a thrilling idea. They had options their parents didn't have anymore.

The carpet of Rach's room was kelly green, like some distant field where gnomes could thrive. Rach was going to be a stewardess. She'd lined up the Star Wars figures into airplane rows and served them Life Savers and Skittles. When they were done she took away their trash.

"I think you've had enough," she said to Darth Vader, who was trying to get an extra mini-bottle of wine. She took away his saber, just in case he got testy.

When Karla moved to Damariscotta with her parents it was a dark day. She gave Rach the freeze-dried ice cream from her Christmas stocking—it would last for millennia.

Karla's father said it would be safer in Damariscotta. He didn't have to explain anymore but he did. The power plant, Maine Yankee, could explode or implode. It was built before they'd figured out what to do with the waste, her father said, which did seem unforgivably stupid, like shitting in a hot tub.

Also, someone could sabotage it. Or something could catch

on fire. There would be sirens and debris. There would be air they shouldn't swallow. The two-lane road in and out of Bay Harbor would be jammed—and they'd have to drive right by the plant to get to I-95.

Her father had bought a small motorboat so they wouldn't have to take the highway. (He paid someone in beer to scrape off the algae and bail out the water in the summer.) There were dry goods in their crawl space, plain cardboard boxes with rubber-stamped words: CHICKEN PARMESEAN, BEEF BARLEY STEW, MACARONI AND CHEESE. More freeze-dried astronaut food. In an emergency, they could carry one cardboard box each. There was an inflatable ten-gallon water jug and a locked-away rifle, because someone with less foresight might want their MAC AND CHEESE.

Her father drove to Augusta each month for Anti-Nuke meetings and wrote letters to the editor. He organized the evacuation procedures at Karla's schools. He distributed the photocopied packets with phone trees and maps. The noontime siren would wail and they'd go to their designated spots.

Karla was in charge of taking the weekly radiation readings. She had to turn on a small black box with a red light, kept on her father's bureau. She counted for sixty seconds. She had to do this three times and average the times together. Then she called someone named Rufus, with a thick Maine accent, and he thanked her kindly. She sometimes forgot to turn off the little black box and her mother would hear the beeps and say, "Red alert," and laugh. The study had been going on for years. How much data did they need?

Her father was not just concerned about these things, but angry too. Nuclear power, Clarence Thomas, welfare reform. Not angry in a scary way, but with enough vehemence for Karla to pay attention to his arguments. She learned to listen to men with clear opinions. He was outlining his disbelief and frustration with dumb, thoughtless human beings and more esoteric evils, like viruses. (Her father hadn't been permitted to take out library books or chew on grass he plucked from the roadside. Someone could have spit right there. He didn't say spit, but expectorate.)

He explained about eggs and salmonella.

He gave her an emergency rope ladder to throw out her bedroom window in case of fire.

"Enough," said Karla's mother. She tried to change the subject. She told Karla about something in the *Times*—a play or an exhibit—which she only read on Sundays, the sections lasting the whole week, *Style* in the bathroom, *Arts and Leisure* by her TV chair. *Auto* used to start the fire. She called ahead to reserve it, her name written in the upper right-hand corner, right next to the weather in Manhattan.

Before the bank took the house in Damariscotta, Karla's parents took her to New York City once a year to see the Rockettes and the Museum of Natural History. They took cabs everywhere because the subway wasn't safe and one time a cabbie wouldn't take them to the Bronx, where Karla's aunt still lived. But her mother yelled at him until he changed his mind.

In New York, her father was quiet and her mother was in charge. She could walk fast and hail taxis and order with confidence in Katz's deli. (Pastrami on toasted rye with a Dr. Brown's cream soda.) Before they went back she bought three packages of Mallomars, which they couldn't get in Maine. At home Karla's mother kept them in Zip-locked bags and allowed herself just two at a time.

There were Yiddish words Karla knew: *schlep, schmuck, schmatte, goyim, chutzpah, bah-rook a toy add an oy.* Her father learned these words too.

"Your mother has *chutzpah*," he said, not always kindly. When she went back to the store for the missing *Book Review* section. When she sent back food that was too cold or too rare or had too much mayonnaise. When she broke up a fight between two summer boys outside the YMCA. When she played Simon Legree in the local production of *The King and I*. When she danced by herself at weddings. She was an excellent dancer. There were pictures of her in a belly dancing costume, her stomach bare and perfect.

She took Karla to dance classes in Portland. *There are creative and inspiring things everywhere*, her mother said in the car. Maybe not as many in Maine as there could be, but they existed. You just had to drive to them.

"See how your neck tips up?" said the modern dance teacher, pressing down on Karla's collarbone. "Think about looking straight ahead."

But Karla didn't know how to correct the angle of her neck. She kept looking up, wanting to catch the view, wanting to be like the tallest pines in her yard. How regal they were. How they stayed, even at an incline. They were important and stately, pushed around by Atlantic winds. There was no deterring them—up, up toward the light. They would be seen. They needed to get fed and they were fed.

She looked up at boys. She learned if you told them too much they ran away. They didn't like the idea of you liking them. Karla forgot this, again and again, or didn't forget but couldn't help herself. Howie Webster. Red hair, thick freckles, arms that were muscled from wrestling. She wanted to scoop him up and dedicate songs to him. Until he started to hide from her in the halls.

It felt good to tell the truth. Why didn't it feel good to hear it?

She didn't get asked to the Jr. High Prom. They thought she was one of those girls who fell in love with anyone she kissed.

That wasn't always true. Howie kissed her, then started writing something in imaginary cursive with a stuffed pillow pencil she'd made in Home Ec. "I" he wrote, smiling at her, looking hard to make sure she understood. "Love" he wrote. And then he dropped the pillow and started humping her madly.

Maybe the last word was going to be humping. He kept rubbing and she knew then she could be an inanimate thing—a log or a washing machine—and he'd feel the same. She was surface area.

She didn't stop being the one they rubbed against. It was easier to say yes. She went with them to Ocean Point to drink beer and to Barrett's Park in flip-flops to wade around the broken glass and rusted lobster traps.

She got a summer job that paid nothing, and from behind the box office window of the Dinner Theatre, Pete Gerard had seemed so different, like a sad, soulful boy, unlikely to hump her too soon. There had been some trouble back in Lewiston but no one knew all the details. His father had done something he shouldn't have. They were French-Canadian. Canucks. He'd moved with his mom to Bay Harbor in fifth grade.

He didn't say much and that was fine, Karla thought. He'd come to the box office window to borrow a pen. Cute and lean, moody-looking. Smelled like the pot he'd just smoked. His jeans hung loose on his waist, and his neck was narrow and soft looking, like a girl's. He had a wispy, black goatee. His arms stuck out of the sleeves in a fragile way. His T-shirt said, "I'd like to buy the world a Coke" and seemed like it had been washed about a billion times.

"You should eat more," Karla said to him. He looked like he didn't always eat. Circles under his eyes. A tiny hoop from Silver Lining in his left ear. Karla was wearing the same one in all four holes. She saw him notice this.

She said, "You look like an actor."

"Because of the earring?"

He had a slow smile. It seemed an effort for him to make it work. "Have you ever?" Karla said, looking at the faded letters.

He looked down at his chest. "Done coke?"

"Bought the *world* one."

She'd thought the dinner theatre boys would be like him—artsy, moody. But they'd mostly paired off with one another, leaving the girls in the cast to drink by themselves at Gray's Pub after work. Karla wasn't old enough to go. Her mother picked her up outside the theater at 11:00 PM, right after Karla had swept the theater floor and swiped down the tables with Windex.

This was supposed to be Karla's penance for flunking out of Lincoln Academy, the better school in the neighboring town twenty minutes away. A job where she wasn't really paid, a curfew that was pointless. She'd wanted to lie about her age and serve cocktails at the Muddy Rudder but her mother thought the theater job was a much better idea. Educational. A Stepping Stone. Her mother picked her up at eleven, and at midnight Karla snuck out to meet Pete at Ocean Point. Soon she brought him to her room when everyone else was at work. It was easy to make him stay inside the cozy, mossy walls. She played *A Chorus Line* and sat in his lap. She kissed him with her tongue.

She described her music teachers at Lincoln Academy. Mr. Steve played "Another Saturday Night" on his guitar, a chorus of them chanting "I got some money 'cause I just got paid" which they turned into "just got laid." Then Mrs. O'Connell replaced him, red-cheeked, kind, the highness of her own voice pushing them to sing out more. The Messiah! In high school! How cool that she'd trusted them enough to try it. The Glee Choir and modest choreography. The *West Side Story* medley.

"Sounds like a good place for that," Pete said. "For music and whatnot."

It had been, she said. Better than Bay Harbor High, where

she'd go in the fall and kick the ass of all the stupid little sopranos wearing windbreakers.

Ten years later, in the Thistle (Rachel hadn't been able to find a sitter; Head Office still hadn't called), Pete's goatee is gone. He has the glazed look of the other non-athletic boys in town who'd married young and stayed put.

Karla watches him walk in and knows what will happen.

She remembers Molly's name of course but not the name of their son, who isn't very old. Karla's mother had sent the *Tribune* birth announcement all the way to the ship's home port of Majorca.

She sips the sweet drinks Pete buys her and talks about the ship. How she tried the wristbands and the shots and still the floral pattern of the Showboat Lounge carpet leapt up at her in bad seas. She drank more. Just one strong gin and tonic, and then when she wobbled it was exactly like having a very good buzz. She tried two gin and tonics—this lasted longer. It was harder to wake up for AM duties, but at least this sickness was her own doing.

"You shouldn't do that," says Pete.

"Shouldn't what?"

"Shouldn't fuck with the ocean."

"No," says Karla.

He looks like he wants to say more.

"But to us He gives the keeping of the light along the shore." she sings. "You know that hymn?"

He does, from Molly, who sang it at the Blessing of the Fleet. Karla sings another verse and a chorus. He snorts when she gets to "seaman."

She admits to Pete that she spent most of her first ship contract blowing up and popping balloons instead of singing songs onstage. In the morning she chased them around with her nametag pin

(*Karla—Entertainer*). This duty happened early because it would be unprofessional to have last night's set still up in the lounge too late into the next day. There were passengers up at that hour, of course, the walkers and the tai chi devotees. They heard the popping and came into the lounge in their spandex to watch Karla on Break Down. She had to smile and explain, or shrug and make a joke. She felt nauseous—it was early and she hadn't eaten and they weren't yet in port, the ship rocking like a whale, the small and constant shifting underneath. Chalky taste of rubber on her lips from replacing old with new.

Then she switches and tells him the story of shooting down the crazy water slide in Dubai. "Wild Wadi." Just a long dark tube leading down. How terrifying it was to fall like that, at first, without knowing when the light and splash would come. But then, because she couldn't get out of it, she had to let it go. Not her problem. *I'm stuck in this and can't get out.* Might as well embrace it. How lovely to not be in control. She'd hurried to line up again.

She had so many stories for him. Even those that hadn't happened yet.

"Everything's the same here," he says. The sun so bright on water. Too much prettiness. Rumors and true stories about accidents and guns. The dentist, caught selling painkillers and fondling his patients in the chair again. They like to think their sweet harbor keeps them immune from things. But it's just like anywhere else.

This disappoints Karla more than she can explain. All the scenic postcards of lobster boats and every other winter someone ends up dead in a smashed car.

"Remember *Pippin*?" says Karla, to change things.

Pete does another shot. He doesn't say anything about Molly, but Karla pictures it anyway. How Molly's voice has begun to grate in their cold house by the water. In bed he knows exactly how she'll jerk and arch. He's already begun to resent his wife—

it's impossible not to.

Pete coughs. They're the only ones left at the Thistle. He pays and helps her with her coat.

The sex at Ocean Point is blurry and fast.

With Pete it will be different. He doesn't talk much, and Karla can fill in the spaces at last. They are the same, she finds out. Inside she's like him—quiet. And inside he's like her—loud.

"Because you look for your mirror," says Rachel. "Everyone does."

It seems less exciting the way she says it.

Does Molly talk a lot too? Does it make Pete less lonely? Molly has tits—and lovely round smells under her blue wool sweater, biscuit and jam-type smells. She's smart. Her lips are full and pretty. She can kiss him hard and mean it. She can laugh from her gut. She can fold his shirts and stack them on a chair beside their bed. She can yell if he comes home drunk. Sometimes, she wants to squeeze him too hard and he has to get away.

She's focused, our Molly, on one thing at a time. That's how she made the Honor Roll. She has the straight-ahead look the dance teacher wanted. She's a Townsend, rooted in, and unlikely, Karla thinks, to waste time chasing the bitch who caused it all.

After the Thistle, Pete and Karla have sex anywhere they can think of—outside in fields and in tents and against trees and he looks at her parts closely, likes to get his nose in. As they drive to secret places, he reaches across and rubs at her from the driver's seat and she looks at the road until everything is rushing, fuzzy.

"You'd like New York," Karla says to him. Which doesn't have to be an invitation if he doesn't want to come.

Maybe he'll leave Molly like so, with the TV still on:

"Going to get a beer. Want anything?"

Molly will finish her stupid show and then the one after, the one she doesn't normally watch, and then she'll wait and listen hard for noises—car door thumping, crunch of gravel. *It's taking him a while.* Her heart will jiggle as the pine boughs snap against the windows. *He just went to the Point for a long drive, to the waves, getting as close to water as he possibly can.* She'll prepare things for nighttime. Dishes, son, clothes for work, busy busy, move the hands. She'll imagine hearing, finally, the frozen ground complaining under heavy, booted feet. She'll open the door and wedge her body between the warmth of the house and the breeze outside, the loudness of wind on water, the chimes clanging from branch. But it isn't him, not yet. *Storm's a-brewing. There could be dead things hanging from trees or there could be nothing, just wind and earth and sea.*

But of course it isn't hard for Molly to be alone. And of course she'll know: He stopped at the Thistle, he's drunk by now, too drunk to come home, but he will come home.

She'll try to sleep. She'll see her sad, worn-out face in the mirror. It will seem impossible that she's become this woman waiting for her husband to come home. She'll feel like the dumb country songs she secretly loves.

She'll be glad for the heavy blanket, some weight on her in the dark. Something to keep her there, pressing down a little.

In the morning she'll know. She'll feel it, the shift in the house and the sea outside. The wind has died. The chimes barely touch. He isn't there anymore. And he isn't coming back, sure as shit.

Maybe she'll be relieved. One less grip of annoyance in her lovely home in the woods. She'll be more likely to succeed.

Karla thinks, *She knows everyone in town. She'll see them at Video City and have to explain. She'll have to smile bravely, standing next to her son.*

People leave all the time—it's just what they do, people you love. It's in Karla's family too, a gene for departure. Everyone jumps ship eventually.

When Karla gets the call, she's in her mother's bathtub, plucking the hairs from her nipples. It isn't Head Office. It's New York City.

"AMDA?" her mother shouts up the stairs. "American Dramatic and Musical Academy?" Karla dries her hands and answers right away, trying to remember which cover letter and why.

She says yes, but she takes her time going back to the city. She has to kick the lawyer out of her apartment. She has to tell more stories to Pete.

Then she takes the bus and the train and the taxi. The bar below her window has become a yoga studio. Someone hands her a flyer for a free class, and she finds she can follow. It's the same poses over and over. They call it a practice.

She starts the job at AMDA as Admissions Associate. Which means she's a telemarketer.

She auditions on days off. *Namaste,* she writes in emails. She buys patchouli. And as though summoned by the scent, Pete answers her postcard, the one with King Kong hitched to the side of the Empire State. *Hi,* she wrote. *Meet me at the Met?*

Will he actually come? A piece of her crappy hometown right there in the big city? She could cook pasta and salads, cookies and pies. She could feed him and feed him and he'd never want to go.

Part Three

Listen,
my wary one, it's far too late
to unlove each other. Instead let's cook
something elaborate and not
invite anyone to share it but eat it
all up very slowly.
—William Matthews, "Misgivings"

The Wife

Copenhagen, 1903

METTE'S PANTRY WASN'T WELL stocked. "Come into my pantry," she said, the one room in the house without windows, and they did—the baker, the fishmonger, the art dealer, more than once. The crusty jam jars knocked closer to the edge with the banging of Mette's hips. She watched the jars jiggle. She wondered if one might fall from the top shelf and crack the head of Schuff.

"You're losing weight," said the dealer, fastening his belt in the pantry. He was gentle—didn't spank or hoot like the baker. Looked at her face a little before he was done.

"Not so much," Mette said, but it was true. She was skipping breakfast, drinking teacups of rusty water to trick her body into nourishment. Saving the eggs for her youngest son.

Schuff followed her gaze to the jars. "Paint?" he said.

"Yes," said Mette. The dried bits her husband hadn't yet rinsed away: teal, chartreuse, vermillion. Shades not found in Denmark.

"Louise made stew," said the dealer.

"No—thank you," said Mette. *Dear God, no more stew from Louise.* She ached from the fucking. She wanted her grandfather's pipe.

"Tomorrow?" said Schuff. He left the *krone* on the table without counting, careful to ignore the faded patch of wall where the Cezanne had been.

"Tomorrow," said Mette, and the front door closed.

If a jam jar fell, if it cracked the head of a jiggler—

She'd have to explain when the coroner came, the lack of trousers, the limp dick coiled, blood seeping into the misshapen sack of flour. The police would find the letters—chalky, sifted. They'd ask, *Madame Gauguin? Wife of the painter?* And she'd be able to tell it all at last. They'd keep asking questions, hungry for details.

We have an arrangement, you see. My idea.

Why had it been it her idea?

Mette checked the clock—the children would be home. She rolled the hashish into a small, hard ball on the cedar desktop, the wood faded and clean. As a girl she'd pictured a house with turrets and secret rooms. A bedroom canopy like a sail. Bejeweled things that didn't need to be: doorknobs, faucets, letter openers.

She did have a letter opener. Plain, dagger-shaped. Not sharp enough to do real harm.

She'd received thirty-eight letters from her husband so far, from Pointoise to Pont-Aven to Le Pouldu, from year to year, with stops back home when he needed more funds. Each trip brought him closer to the sea. Splashing around with paint with acquaintances from the bank, at first. Then, when Europe was no longer appealing, when Vincent was dead and Theo insulted, the envelopes said "Panama," "Martinique," "Oceania"—*Oceania.* It seemed like a made-up place. But the stamps proved it. Floral, ornithological, the kind Mette's mother had peeled and kept in book. Petals in funny angles like pretty orange cunts.

Gone for two years this time. *Yes, Officer, two. Just look at the stamps.*

She considered the Pissaro oil, the *tiki* sketches from Papeete.

The chipped, mahogany chairs with the knotted claws for arms—her own wrists thicker. The stool near the pantry, a footprint on the pale pink seat.

She felt under her drawers, damp from Schuff. She smoothed the skirt evenly over her thighs. She lit the pipe and breathed until her mind became a flat, gray sea.

Mette first kissed her husband on the beach at Le Havre, that summer in France without her parents, the ships inching in, the water steely and frigid, even in the height of summer. She'd beaten him easily, swimming a portion of the bay—neat, sure strokes, her lungs good and tired. They sat together in the tepid sun to dry. At night, under the pier, Paul smelled like clean sheets and he wore a felt cap with a brown brim, a hat too old for him. It fell to the sand, and he clasped himself to her like a pin.

He tried to teach her about his palette, testing her at the shore. *Look at the water. What colors do you see?* She didn't have all the words in French. She distracted him with touches and whispered to him in Danish. He said he liked the stops and starts of her language. The sure, spitting sound.

A man should have a hobby, she'd thought at the time. It meant he had something to talk about besides the bank. Didn't she have hobbies too? The chorale. Her solo in the *Messiah*. How lovely if that had been the thing to define her.

She'd come to France as a governess because her parents approved—such a wealthy family she boarded with. They didn't know about the evenings at the theater, the Montmartre cafés, the nights with Paul. "I could crush you," he'd said. (*Not likely*, she'd thought, *you scrawny little thing.*) It had been pleasing to be twisted. He liked the fleshiest parts of her, the haunch and sag. He grabbed on and pressed hard, leaving marks. How beautifully slight and small he was—it was sometimes possible for Mette to imagine he was a girl.

This was when he sketched her still, when he loosened her silk robe to trace her outlines. He dipped his hand in his palette, smearing the colors on her shoulders, her thighs. Handprints on her back like a messy child, the silk ruined, and how little it mattered.

To pass the time she painted too that summer. Not the vistas but a fairy tale she'd read as a child about a mermaid growing legs, becoming what the sailor wanted her to be. More in his image. The confusion and the joy, mixed. She wasn't herself any longer.

The painting was sloppy—no shading, few details. Blotches of color. Mette didn't care. She wasn't trying to impress him, she was just giving shape to what was in her mind at the time.

But he was trying to impress her. He looked at it for a long while on the beach. He added a stroke here, a curve there, without asking if he could.

"Don't," she laughed. "It's mine."

He didn't stop. "C'est mieux," he said when he was done.

It was better. A record of their time together by the sea.

He proposed in the middle of August, just before she was meant to go back to Copenhagen. And so she didn't go back.

They stayed in France together for years—until almost all the children were born.

The first journey away from France had been Mette's idea, once Paul's job at the exchequer fell through. *There are banks in Copenhagen too*, she'd said. He could dig in somewhere new, a place that was hers. The children could learn her language and know their grandparents well. Paris wasn't impossibly far away when he had the urge for his own city.

"*Something's rotten in the state of Denmark*," he'd said. Something icy in his tone, which made it hard for Mette to laugh.

In Copenhagen he cared less about banking, more about his hobby. He took a trip to Paris just three months after the move to discuss a potential exhibit at the Salon. Two weeks stretched to four.

Complicated business, this Art World, he wrote. *The Salon is filled with snobbery and backward thoughts about the Impressionists. Tell the children I'll bring them Parisian treats.*

It will pass, Mette thought. He'll return to the bank after the Salon.

But the following summer he spent two months in Brittany with a colleague called Emile Schuffenecker, another banker turned artist, *though not the painter I am*, her husband wrote.

Then—*Salon be damned. The Breton women wear the most extraordinary headgear. Giant flaps of white—like wings! Their simplicity is refreshing, a kind of primitive belief in faith and love.*

Mette hadn't replied right away. What did headgear have to do with faith? What did painting have to do with it?

The descriptions of the peasant women grew more detailed—the curves of their shoulders, their long, shapely necks. Paul decided to spend August there as well—his friend Vincent had joined him, and the fat Madame Ginoux was most generous about the lodging fee. The season changed, and with it the hotel rates—cheaper still. He'd even met a man who'd seen New England.

America, Australia, the West Indies—every far-flung coast called to him. He wrote about a small circle of turf that had loosened itself from the shore in Massachusetts. Vincent had told him—an island adrift somewhere in the Atlantic. *Just imagine, Mette! An island that floats* to *you.*

She tucked the letter back in and tried to focus on her needlepoint. Another pillow for little Pola to cling to and stain.

Just think how much further I could go, he meant.

The first mention of Tahiti came in October: *May the day come (soon perhaps) when I'll flee to the woods on an island in Oceania, there to live in ecstasy, calm, and art. With a new family by my side, far from this European scramble for money. There, in Tahiti, in the silence of the beautiful tropical nights, I'll be able to listen to the soft murmuring of my heart in harmony with the mysterious beings around me. Free at last, without financial worries and able to love, sing and die."*

Mette didn't read too closely. She saw "new family" and something about finances. She began to think of Tahiti as a germ, a place that infected. Or maybe Paul was the germ, right there in their home. He had to get himself far away.

Between letters, he bounced the mattress hard. She felt a yanking in her brain, like grass being ripped out by the roots. Then he snored out his absinthe breath, filling the room with it. He woke again at dawn—bleary, confused. He parted the sheet cocoon she'd made and pulled her nightgown up again. She moved her hips. He didn't kiss her, and she felt how heavy she was, how little she distracted him.

Sometimes, as pink light wormed through, as the horses started to grunt and clomp in the street, she tried to kiss him before he could turn his mouth away.

She'd still had the will to ask questions, then. She remembered when they'd been walking along the canal and the wind was very sharp. She'd tucked her hands into her own pockets to warm them, rather than use the heat of the man beside her.

"Why?" she'd asked. *Why are we like this now?*

"I don't know," he'd said. "I'll have to think about that." His face was slack, his levity gone. She couldn't read him, couldn't see if this was a diversion or if he really didn't know.

Years later he still hadn't figured it out—the "why" of not kissing her. Or maybe he just hadn't gotten back to her about it.

She grew to appreciate the cool patches of sheet in his absence. She could fling her leg over to hit—nothing. She'd sealed herself off like a wick tucked under wax. It would be hard to dig her back out again. So many mornings—Mette made herself remember—the weight of her husband had kept her tethered there, the pull to be upright countered by his arm across her waist. She'd kept her eyes open and listened to the pipes cracking against the wind, the house shifting, the boards pinned together and moaning. Not unlike the cabin of a ship.

From Papeete he'd written, *Farewell, dear Mette, dear children. Love me, and when I'm back we will get married again. Which means, today I'm sending an engagement kiss to you.*

She'd un-love her husband in increments.

She felt this was the kindest way, given the children. It wouldn't do for them to think of their father as a jackass. He was a jackass. But it wouldn't do for them to know it all at once.

She read all the letters. She flung only one into the stove, glad to hear it crackle. She kept the rest deep in the flour sack, the ones about "*tiki* statues of chocolate wood" and "sunsets of blood orange." The stories he wanted to tell in pictures; why he'd decided to become a Symbolist. To Schuff he sent the blank Tahitian faces to sell, their limbs like Christ or Buddha. Splotches of plain color where he's once taken such care with shading.

"It's an idea he has," Schuff said, not in the pantry. "It isn't about the vistas anymore. The pretty places help him, of course—they carry him for short bursts at his easel."

Mette smeared the dishcloth in useless circles around the good China plate. "The savages believe this?" she offered. "Beauty to inspire ugliness?"

But Schuff was already lost in numbers and didn't reply. He'd examined the canvases carefully. Two this time. He was about to calculate their commission with her best fountain pen.

It helped that Mette was good with negotiations too.

As a child she'd gathered up her dolls at Christmastime, an odd bouquet of tiny limbs poking out of their velvety dresses. She wrapped them back up in their tissue, even the ones she might have grown attached to, and carried them to the schoolyard to sell.

"Where are your presents?" her mother had said.

"I gave them away." Mette watched as her mother's face did a complicated leap from surprise to suspicion.

"How kind of you," said her mother, her mouth twisted unkindly. "Perhaps—in future—there won't be any toys."

But the next year there were more toys, more dolls. "Thank you, Mother. Thank you, Father," Mette had said. And then sold them all again.

Better, she'd thought, *than cracking the porcelain faces with Father's hammer and tossing the flakes around the dying balsam tree.* Why did she have the urge to do this? She couldn't say. She just wanted to be older, away from their rigid ideas about who she was permitted to be.

In Copenhagen, she pared down the house to the things she needed: stove, couch, bookshelf, desk, pantry. She saved the nice china, the glasses, just in case. She sold Paul's private collection piece by piece. Schuff said the money for the Cezanne was coming, plus the money from Paul's last batch. They only had to get the book published, the Stink Stink book—*Noa Noa*—and then there'd be plenty of *krone* for all. Schuff needed a way to explain it to buyers—the young girls and blobs of color.

With Schuff she had the prospect of cash, at least. And vats of Louise's mealy stew.

She remembered the time Schuff retrieved Paul from the alley in Montmartre—the look Schuff had given her at the door. *What a mess of a husband you have,* reeking of opium and sweat. Paul had lost his coat, the kerchief around his neck stained with brown—paint or dried fluid. Mette had wondered, briefly, if it had been the whore's menstrual blood or if something more insidious had happened.

How easy it had been, the first time in the pantry with Schuff. When he'd left, Mette stuffed the pipe with the waxy resin Paul had forgotten and felt again like a daring girl, a good swimmer.

Mette's sister came to Copenhagen and bought marzipans shaped like apples. At night the two drank sherry and discussed the pain in her sister's knee, the money their father refused to give Mette until she left the *Fransk artist-schmuck* for good.

Mette didn't miss her husband at these times.

"He's testing you," said her sister. "Naked girls with fruit?" She plucked at a dangling thread from the arm of the sofa.

"He's taken their beliefs," said Mette, unable to stop herself.

"Fine, yes." said the sister. "But why so many tits?"

The women looked at each another for a moment and then broke it—loud laughter in the big, drafty house.

"I have to explain it somehow," said Mette.

Her sister nodded and wiped her eyes with her sleeve.

When the subsequent letters arrived, Mette would feel nothing but a tiny, distant quark in her throat.

He wrote, *My studio is very handsome and I can assure you time goes by quickly...What a pity you have not tasted this Tahitian life; you would never want to live any other way.*

When he was sick he wrote more often: *I'm spitting blood—a small bucket's worth...and my hospital treatment is twelve francs per day.*

She skimmed, until—

I'm soon to be the father of a half-caste; my charming Dulcinea has decided to lay an egg.

The paper was light brown, as though made of finely ground twigs. The stamp was from somewhere called Mataiea.

Pola found it, digging in the flour. "Mumma."

"Give it," said Mette. Her son's hand was cool and small.

"Is it the pirates?" he said. "Have they let Papa go?"

She smacked him on the bottom for looking at her things, harder than she meant to. The flour on his hands left pawprints on the old, striped couch.

Again Schuff waved the telegram like a flag in her living room. Mette's insides thumped—a thick fear of becoming unglued again.

Home in a fortnight! Schuff said. With paintings!

She could cast her husband out for good this time, take Pola to her parents. Bury the wick completely.

But the house would be full: Aline, Clovis, and Jean-Rene back from their boarding schools. Emile home from Stockholm. Pola, who said he'd forgotten the exact shade of his father's eyes. (Mette couldn't tell anyone, not even her sister, but she liked Pola best.)

It would be, at least, a time of no letters.

For three days, Paul—cheekbones jutting, his eyes brighter—circled Mette like a slick sea creature, seeming to focus only on the children, petting them, praising them, saying their full names out loud, rewarding them with faded shells and batiks.

Well done, Mette thought. *You remember us at last.*

And then he focused on her too. (*Is this what she missed? Being looked at closely?)* In bed he took his time. He was thrilled with her ass again, her sturdy legs. His mouth was turned away, but sometimes she found she could arouse herself, by planting herself on him solidly. (*And what if she was to slide off his stiff prick and be done?)* She let her full weight press into him (he'd lost so much weight), felt him shift and begin to be smothered.

I could crush you, she thought. And flipped her full weight back down beside.

When Paul had been drinking and couldn't manage anything else, he stroked her hair—the length of her head, feeling for bumps in her skull, the unseen parts of her. Just as she'd seen him stroke the flanks of dogs, making them fall sleep from the pleasure in being touched.

She wasn't able to sleep herself, but she allowed the hand to crack her open. She let the wick poke though, just enough to keep her there, despite the daylight calling her into other rooms.

In the pantry Paul rooted around for the scraps in the jelly jars, the ocean shades, the pantry where Schuff had fucked her against the shelves. If she told him this, would they be even? Would he want to claim her, stay for good? Or would he stab Schuff with his canvas knife and leave again?

Maybe Paul already knew. Maybe Schuff had written to him after absinthe, the guilt stewing. Or maybe Paul had encouraged Schuff to do it outright.

I've known you for so long, her husband had written from Papeete. Which was not quite the same as *I miss you*. He didn't apologize, but he became aggressively happy at home, as though he'd long ago come to terms with his trespasses. The small squabble of leaving. *Get over it, Mette.* As though she'd been unfaithful too, for doubting.

Months passed. They sat together on the drooping couch while Pola slept. Paul drank port from the crystal glasses, the ones Mette never took out, the ones he used even for milk and water when he was home. He swirled the glass, a purple drip sloshing onto his hand, which he licked just in time. He wiped the sticky streak on the throw pillow.

She didn't say, "Careful—it will stain." She listened. She wanted the sourness rising up to fall swiftly back down.

"I think I'm done with this," said her husband. He looked around the bare, dusty room.

A nerve throbbed under Mette's eye.

But she knew he meant the sad, rumpled furniture that remained—the dark corners. The holes in the house from the fights they'd had. (A puncture on the wall, fist level. A low pock from the force of his shoe on light wood. The splinters of paintbrush she'd snapped, still lodged in the floorboard cracks.) They were too old to be living like this, he meant. Too smart to pretend it was romantic, all this decay. In Tahiti it would be one thing, but here—

"Just how long will you be with us?" Mette asked, to cut to the center quickly. "And when will the money come?"

He said he had plans for the bookcase (too small) and the writing desk (too old). He wanted flower pots for the window sills.

His voice in that room. *Smashing her perfect dolls.* She opened her throat, about to let herself become a different creature—

"I could take the children," he said. What an adventure they would have! It would be good for them to feel the sun and the water and learn about the world beyond Denmark.

She waited. She counted seconds, then breaths. Perhaps they

would speak more productively, she found herself saying, away from the dirty rooms. Perhaps along the canal.

But they didn't move.

She could go. She could walk away and sail, leaving the pantry too. For a moment she saw this option before her clearly.

And then she was back on the sofa with her husband.

He didn't answer. He reached for more port and filled the glass too high. It tipped and dripped again as he brought it to his mouth, leaking onto his mustache and his beard, splashing the carpet. He didn't rise to clean it.

Much, much later, Mette would remember that evening and wonder about his intentions. Maybe it was the only way he could say it. *Listen to my plans, Mette. I have plans for us.* A vow of sorts.

That evening she focused on the sex, the head petting, which did make her less irritated by morning. She wore a white blouse buttoned up high, her hair in a soft, careful bun, a cameo pin at her neck. She went to the market and the spring air made the streets smell like salt and lilacs. At the butcher's (he winked) she bought liver and kidney, the same parts ailing in her husband, the doctor had said. She would make a pate. She'd spend the afternoon with her hands in foodstuff, mashing in.

He wasn't there when she returned, but still she pounded the parts together in a large, chipped bowl. When the clock said ten o'clock she set the cameo brooch facedown on her desk, a distinct, hard click. Gone for breakfast, lunch, and dinner. A full two days.

Then: bruised, foul-smelling. The pocket of his wool tweed pants torn off. Patchy gray beard on his face. Her heart rattled. Relief at seeing him alive.

Please, he said in the bath. *We don't have to live like this!*

She scrubbed at his back. *True*, she said. *And if you stay here I will have to hurt you, badly. If our children continue to starve I promise I will cut you with the butcher knife.*

A week later he set sail again.

She hadn't meant it. He knew that. Needed his *tikis,* his *vahines.* Remembered the names of his children on that continent too. *Aline and Emile. Same as their dead daughter and their eldest, which was also the same as his closest friend.* How much he must care for Schuff to do such a thing.

She left the pate rotting in the icebox until Pola complained.

She tried to read from *The Complete Works of Shakespeare* without bracing for him. She made herself hear the honest quiet in their home.

But in daylight it was hard to ignore the evidence in the plain face of her youngest son.

"Where is he?" said Pola.

"He's with us in spirit. Just his body is very far."

"He's dead?"

"He's not dead. He's painting."

"He could paint here."

"He has to live far away from us. He's very sick."

"So he's going to die soon."

"Not soon, but of course he's going to die. We all die." She tucked his hair behind his ear, and he ran away from her with his milk.

There were no letters from Oceania for very long time.

On a used envelope, her husband had once written a note that was a question, a request: *Mette, will you return?* It was propped beside a stack of Royal Library books on Greek *kouros* and Javanese temples.

She'd returned the books of course. She'd kept the slip of paper and placed it deep in the desk drawer. She pretended now that the request was unrelated to books.

Mette, will you return?

Because he'd taught her about color—or tried to. He'd made her see in a way she couldn't on her own. *It's just sea and sky,* she'd thought, when he'd asked her to name what she saw in Le Havre. But everything was italicized with him. She didn't have to italicize things herself.

Their last kiss—when had it been exactly? When had it last felt like they'd been in agreement? She tried to remember at her desk, flapping her skirt to cool herself, sticky again from Schuff.

It was before his first trip to Brittany. How carefully he'd packed his easel, his colors. How hopeful and sad he'd looked at the door. *This could be the last time I see him*, Mette had thought—even then, seventeen years ago—kissing her husband goodbye.

The relief she'd felt. And then the surprise of missing him as soon as he was out of view. A moment of panic, forgetting how to light the stove. *She had to light the stove.*

And then she was able to light the stove.

At least now he wasn't there to not kiss her. He wasn't there not kissing her on the sofa.

Now he was in a place called Hiva Oa. Or so the last letter indicated, the one she hadn't yet opened. A stamp with a blue orchid, "Gauguin" scrawled in the left-hand corner in the way it always was. The loop of the second "g" larger than necessary. It occurred to her, he could be anywhere—hiding out, the next street over!—were it not for his letters. His alibis.

But how could she know for sure? On the docks of Le Havre, for the price of postage: *Do me one small favor, mon ami? Mail this letter from Oceania?*

The pipe made her lungs feel like she'd been swimming. She pinched and rolled another ball. Minutes now before Pola came back. She took off her shoes, unpinned her hair, made a little pile of clips in a white China bowl. She picked a pin up and dug her gums with it, pinched her tongue, her nose, her nipple through the nightgown, which hurt some.

She thought of an island knocking into her, hard. Bumping up by pleasant surprise.

She thought of what to pack if she had to pack quickly, just one small bag. Underwear, toothbrush, comfortable shoes, and stockings. A book. Maybe two. A dress? Would she need to look presentable? Would she need to charm and impress? But with the dress, she'd need nice shoes and pins for her hair. Her best earrings, the choker that matched. Her cameo. Powder for her face. And perfume—would she be able to bathe often? Would she need cooking supplies—a pan and some matches, a stick of butter, a loaf of bread? Jars of things that wouldn't spoil? A lemon to prevent scurvy?

Paul had once written an entire page about scurvy. How his mother had it on the ship to Peru—his mother a widow halfway through the crossing. Paul just a boy, younger than Pola. His father's dead body pushed over the side; his mother not eating a thing.

She tried to remember Paul's face vividly, the creases and pocks. The ridiculous beard, the stains on his trousers.

She held the final letter in her hand and felt a strange warmth from her belly up. Her eyes watered from the feeling.

My dear Mette, the letter began, and the barky, twiggy page seemed like an artifact from a distant time.

How are you? Please tell me.

The rest was blank—a page for her to fill in and return.

She tore a triangle from the bottom corner, a slip the length of her finger. She crumpled it tight and placed it on her tongue. *Unlove.* She chewed and chewed, then swallowed.

She tore again, a neat triangle. She swallowed.

When she was done she went to the kitchen and poured a glass of milk. Then another for Pola, who'd come back to her any second.

When she woke, she remembered. Her painting by the shore at Le Havre. Not a painting of the beach at all but a mermaid story. A premonition of a woman adapting to landlock.

In the closet the weight of his art books had make the top shelf loose. But it was there, rolled neatly with string. Untouched since their first summer in France.

She'd been sentimental, once, thank god.

She unfurled the paper on the wooden table, held the corners down with jars. So rough. So blocky and unrefined. But distinct marks where he'd taken over, forced his brush. Defined the mermaid's curves and limbs as he wanted them to be.

She hadn't signed it of course. Why would she?

She could certainly sign her husband's signature now.

How pleased Schuff would be. How much he'd want to believe. *Evidence! His earliest work as a Symbolist.*

She'll tell him to make the funeral arrangements, as per Paul's request. *Upon his death.* Surely his death was upon them. She'd let it be so. Let the dreadful *Savage* monument stand in Oceania, which his Danish children would never have to see.

Molly

New England, 2003

1

"I HAVE TO GET back to the island," Molly Townsend's husband says, like a pledge he's been forced to recite. He scratches at his beard. He smells like he needs a shower.

"You should," says Molly. She stirs cinnamon and raisins into unsweetened oatmeal and doesn't bother looking up at Pete's face again.

"I think I will," says her husband, pecking out the sounds, beaky and sharp. She listens until his boots thump down the stairs to his easel.

If he goes, how calm it will be for an afternoon—no lurking in the basement, Emmett napping. The girls from the bank could come over for nibbles and wine.

(Nibbles? And which girls? Who does she really want to see?)

Back to the island, he said. Last time on Monhegan, a day trip for their anniversary, they had overpriced crab rolls, fog burning off as the ferry tied up, both of them buzzed already on Shipyard Ale. In the museum they looked at pictures of the hermit who'd lived in a shack with his sheep. They peeked in the boarded up windows of the house on Fish Beach where Pete's great-great grandmother had apparently lived. They hiked to Burnt Head, where a bearded fellow stood with a parrot on his shoulder, both bird and man still as stone. "It's a good place for crazy," Pete said.

Yes, it is. Molly mops up oatmeal flakes. Cinnamon powder on the table like some kind of fairy dust. Her chubby son quick and happy with his spoon.

Pete keeps his word. A week later, he squeezes Emmett too long and pats Molly on the arm. He bubble-wraps his easel and goes. He doesn't say when he'll be back.

But he does come back, just before dawn. A day trip only. They don't talk about it for a very long time.

2

PETE'S FAMILY DOESN'T OWN anything on Monhegan now but Molly's family owns things in Bay Harbor—the shipyard and the motel, on the common. The restaurant where Pete likes to have his breakfast. The waitresses look like they're on a movie set, pink gingham aprons over starched, short dresses. A prissy meal, they probably think, of Pete's white toast and tea.

"You'd think we'd eat for free," Pete says.

"It doesn't work that way," says Molly. *Now that I've changed my name for you.*

Her maiden name is on plaques all around town: the indoor track at the YMCA, the pediatric wing at St. Andrew's, the flood lights for the football field, the land trust trails slinking through Oven's Mouth Preserve. Molly's home is the Original Townsend Homestead, used as a summer cottage for years on the tip of Townsend Gut, a slice of extra land jutting out down a long, dark driveway lined with tall pines. The windows rattle in strong winds. The extra insulation and the woodstove help some, but there are times in the dead of January when the gusts slap against the living room walls and push against the low ceiling beams. The wind scares Emmett, who knows all about the Three Little Pigs.

"No one's huffing," Molly tells him, and tucks the flap of his Muppets shirt over the perfect bowl of his belly.

There is no family fortune, she told her husband early on. There's nothing to be grabbed at and wasted.

They could sell the house and not work for a long while, Pete reminds her from time to time.

But in summer the ground is soft with pine needles, orange and dead, hiding turd-sized cones. Molly likes to walk out there barefoot and feel the quiet thump of earth underneath. She can sneak around the perimeter of her family's land and not be heard at all. The rocks slope down, weathered granite worn by salt. There's a spot where her whole body can fit without rubbing against anything jagged. Her son stretches out beside her, and she reckons four of him would make up one of her.

At low tide, the seaweed clumps around the furthest, blackest rocks, and Emmett grabs fistfuls. He likes the kelp pods, slimy inside as they pop. He looks for crabs and squeals when he finds them. They're fast and cooked-looking, yellow, just the size of his big toe. *Watch yourself*, says Molly because it's slippery there, especially under the rockweed bunches where the algae is fresh and gooey.

Across the bay stands a small cluster of houses. Molly flings her arm back and forth, and they do the same. She could scowl and wave and they wouldn't know the difference. She doesn't do this but she's tempted sometimes.

When the wind picks up, the panes get chalky with sea spit, like the fake snow at Christmas, sprayed on windows in town at Wheeler's Drug. It's Pete's job to rub the house windows clean but Emmett likes the snow look, year-round. Come winter they string the smallest pine tree with white lights. It bothers Emmett to see his mother high on the ladder. "It'll look good when it's done," she tells him. Pete grips the length of lights below, keeping them untangled. He sometimes makes faces to distract his son. From across the bay the wavers can see the single white lined tree and know their neighbors are festive, merry people, if not thrifty with electric bills.

"Good fences make good neighbors," her husband says. He surprises her like this, comes out with things she's long forgotten, like the poems they learned for Ms. Patrick. She helped him memorize, tested him, explained what the words meant—how building a fence wasn't a neighborly thing to do at all.

Molly likes to think the best of people, though. She thinks the good thing first and then doubts it later. That's probably the biggest difference between them. Molly thinks they're waving. Pete thinks they're drowning. They'd memorized that poem too.

Such a wizard when he feels like it. Reading books and taking pictures and keeping his secrets pushed far down. Molly catches them on his face sometimes, thoughts trying to come up. He's a puzzle to unlock, Pete the painter, a tricky one. She has to keep working to make the letters fit in the grid.

Once, bored and nervous at the dentist's, she read a *New Yorker* story, the *Vogue* and *People* taken. It was a story about having "a suitable insanity." All men had one, apparently, such as "devotion to a ball team" or a favorite beer. But for the writer (or the person the writer pretended to be in the story—Molly realized there might be a difference, though she doubted it), beer or sports weren't insane enough. To be suitable, the insanity had to be a deeper. It had to be something that took a very long time to understand.

Pete has that, she knows. There are parts of him that are deep and insane—parts that aren't hers to know. At least not yet. She's nothing if not determined.

What's insane about her? What's suitable? Her name, maybe. Molliane. She wanted to be Rosie, a name easy to remember and spell. She remembered how it came to her, staring at her Wonder Woman nightlight, the illuminated circle of her cramped, blue room. Rosie was a flirty, cotton candy kind of name, billowy and sweet. Everyone would want to feel the letters in their mouths.

But at school she found she was still listed as Molliane Townsend, daughter of Will and Val, sister to Megan and Mary Jean.

"Molly Anne?" The teacher paused as she looked at the roster, recognizing the last name of course but not the first.

"Just Molly," said Molly, losing her nerve.

"Oh it's *you*!" said the teacher. "Molly!"

The boy next to her, who would become the town Post Master, ate the booger he'd just picked.

When she was ten, her grandfather gave her a copy of *Ulysses*, a musty volume with tiny print and specks of faded, gold lettering on the spine. It was raining and Molly was trapped, her parents not yet back from the Maine Mall, her sisters at JV practice.

"There's a Molly in this book, Molly Bloom," her grandfather said. He was lean and gnarled, ancient as long as she'd known him. When he wasn't reading or quoting Latin phrases no one knew, he whistled opera songs with a loud, wobbly vibrato. His hearing aid chirped.

"You'll like it," he said. "There's a reader's guide for it somewhere." He adjusted his teeth and read a long passage in a voice that sounded like Henry Higgins from "My Fair Lady." Why was he was talking that way? The book didn't seem to be about a Molly, but a man named Leopold, who apparently enjoyed the smell of his shit.

"He's relieving himself," he grandfather summarized in his cracked, normal voice.

She could understand the pleasure in this, but it seemed a weird thing to include in a book with gold letters. She took the book home. She looked at the last page sometimes and wondered why there were no periods or commas. Then she left it in her shelf for a decade.

Who was she named for really? She'd never thought to ask. And how had her parents become so Irish? If anyone ever asks, she'll tell them she was named for Molly Bloom, an Irish lady and a singer, someone who said YES a lot. The love of Leopold's life.

"You wanted to be Rosie," her father says every now and then. "Thankfully, you forgot."

She didn't forget. The way the letters unfold wasn't how she wanted to be anymore. She just made the ghost of that sugary girl disappear.

She wishes for French speakers in her family, like Pete. They were full-fledged Canucks on his side, all the way back to Antoinette (now that was a name), whom everyone called Toni, the daughter from the shacky house on Fish Beach with a father who'd disappeared. Raised alone by her non-Canuck mother Elizabeth, whom everyone called Lizzie, at a time when women didn't raise girls alone. Lizzie could crack open live lobsters with her bare hands and fish for tuna all alone in stormy seas. They lived in a house that had been dragged through the bay on a big barge, Bay Harbor to Monhegan. No wonder it looked so shacky.

That's all Pete seems to know about it, though Molly has questions. *What happened to Antoinette? What happened to Lizzie? How did they get off island? How did your family end up in Lewiston?*

There's a book Pete inherited, from this Lizzie supposedly, one so crusty and brown it makes Molly cough when she gets too close. Wrinkled pages from being kept close to the sea, a French-English dictionary. It's ruined and sickly, carrying bad spores, but Molly isn't allowed to throw it away.

She opens it sometimes, holding her breath. Inside the front cover is a long paragraph in flashy handwriting, the same word all the way across and down: *MetteMetteMetteMetteMette.*

3

WHEN PETE CAME TO BAY Harbor Elementary in grade five he became known as the boy who did unexpected things. In Math he shouted, "*Je ne sais pas! Je ne sais pas!*" and everyone laughed at him, though they hadn't known the answer either. In gym he had to sit out after whacking the dodge ball straight at Missy Perkins' face.

He could shift from high to low fast, Molly saw. He could make the weather change.

That was the year Molly was 1st runner up in the Ms. Shrimp Princess Pageant. For the talent part she put on a wig and sang "Tomorrow" from Annie. She should have won. Even the winner, a tap dancer, had said so. The 2nd runner up had mimed a Robert Frost poem. Someone else was a hula hooper. But Molly's small, pert boobs had stuck out of her red dress in a way that wasn't shrimpy. She was already too grown up to be Princess.

They were all allowed to ride on the Shrimp Pageant Float, where their legs were wrapped in a black garbage bags. The theme was Mermaids. It was hot, and the bag was tight, so Molly ripped it off on Townsend Avenue and walked up the street to her uncle's motel.

"Sore loser," said the tap dancer.

The other Fisherman's Festival events included trap hauling, tall tales, tug of war, lobster eating, clam shucking, net mending, and bubble gum blowing. There were lobster boat races and a crate-running competition, where the skinnier sternmen hopped from one floating trap to another. The record, held by tiny Mac Michaels, was 340 crates in a row before falling in. Back in a poorly lit corner of the YMCA, the Fisherman's Festival Art Club Prizes were on display.

Molly's favorite part was Roll Call, held at the Fisherman's Memorial, a cast iron, empty rowboat opposite the Catholic Church. All those rugged men and boys, swept up, their names read out by the minister. It made her feel heavy inside to hear them all, but it was at least a calmer feeling than at the fish races. When she was old enough she sang with the school choir. That year Mrs. O. chose "Brightly Beams," her father's favorite hymn. The soprano part was easy enough to follow.

Then she dropped Chorus for Field Hockey, which both her sisters had played. She liked the time before and after games, the focused, serious expressions of her teammates, the way they rolled up socks over their shin guards like knights. They were burly girls, the opposite of shrimpy. But the game itself was long and dull and, because Molly was on the aluminum bench through most of October, quite cold.

She dropped Field Hockey for Art Club. It was warmer and there were moody, quiet boys down there in the basement. The windows were just above ground level, so high up they needed a special pole to unlock them. In winter the windows were often frozen shut from snow. It felt dim, despite the pretty lamps Ms. Barker had brought in. Molly liked the smell—paint and glue—the cave-like space, the silence under the rush of the heat blowing in. A mobile made of real, dead starfish spun and spun.

They had to paint "sea assemblages," as Ms. Barker called them, which were more dead things from low tide like sea urchins and bits of old rope and cracked lobster buoys. Ms. Barker was originally from Wisconsin and still found these things interesting. Molly waited for one of the boys to recognize the colored stripes on the buoy's stem and claim it as his dad's.

But it was good to stare at stuff and draw, good to focus on small objects for a while. She liked the idea of shading, of making things lifelike, and she began to think that Art was something she could do. They were everywhere in Maine—artists. They made pottery or had little shed-sized galleries on roads far from the sea. They went out to Monhegan for a week to stand on the cliffs and drink wine from plastic cups and wonder a little about the native people who'd lived there, butchered by John Smith's men.

Artists had to have other jobs during the winter, her father said, like teaching or waiting tables. They didn't have health insurance, and their clothes were often ill-fitting. "Just look at poor Ms. Barker," he said. She had to mow lawns, come July.

But Ms. Barker was allowed to keep a whole closet of random things down there: wooden knobs, snail shells, dried flowers----the things most people threw away or stepped on without thinking. No one called her a packrat or a crazy lady. The walls were collaged with museum posters and student work and swathes of textured fabrics. There was wrapping paper with Chinese characters and paint chips from Grover's Hardware. It made Molly dizzy to look at it all sometimes.

If she managed a space like that herself she'd at least keep the shelves labeled. She'd wear entirely different work clothes. Ms. Barker favored batik scarves and loose tunics and no bra, which was another reason why the Club was filled with boys.

Pete was the star student, his drawings taking up space on the walls. A quiet boy, French to boot. Molly sat beside him in the basement, watching him handle the glue gun. Her assemblages were lopsided, but maybe he would teach her. He'd painted the Community Mural at the Y and the windows of Burger King at Easter. He'd won the Fisherman's Festival prize.

If she married him there would be paintings everywhere, cluttering their walls. He'd take her to his studio to see his works in progress, and they'd fall onto feather pillows, paint streaking. "It's because of you that I paint," he'd say, "my patient, lovely muse."

She was busy with a string of words for him but resolved not to use them yet.

"Pass me the glue stick?" he said. Then nothing, all through spring.

4

IN THE SUMMERTIME, MOLLY worked at a new age store that sold crystals and incense and whale music (Caribbean whales—warmer, more likely to sing, she guessed). There had to be incense burning and whales singing at all times. The owner installed a barcode detector and reminded Molly to watch out for shoplifters. Why someone would want to steal his incense, she had no idea. Then he revealed the back closet, where the water bongs and pipes were stored.

She was allowed to wear the crystals and energizing stones as long as she remembered to return them to their cases before she left. He paid her in cash, six dollars an hour, which was two dollars more than most places.

Kids came in, busloads of campers on daytrips with five bucks to spend. They walked in lines down Townsend Avenue in matching T-shirts (Camp Wawenock, Camp Cobbosseecontee, Camp Abenaki). The counselors were Molly's age and tired-looking, with obvious packs of cigarettes in their back pockets.

"It stinks in here," said the campers. They imitated the whales. They asked what they could buy for fifty cents, having spent the rest already. For forty cents plus tax they could buy a sticker of the name of the store, which they clapped onto their T-shirts and probably forgot to take off before laundry day. Forty cents seemed steep for a sticker. It was good advertising, the owner said.

"What's behind the curtain?" they asked. The sign said, Must Be 18 To Enter.

"Nothing," she said. Or, "Dead people," which made them want to see it more.

Then Pete came in, and she let him pull back the curtain.

Later that summer, when Pete picked her up from work and took her to the Point, he said she smelled like a Phish concert. He kissed her, letting his hands creep under her polo shirt, which felt nice. She forgot about the whales and the campers.

At the end of the summer, instead of a bonus, the owner gave Molly a book called *Finding the Light: Daily Affirmations* by Shakti Gawain. The author photo revealed a small, elfin woman laughing on a bleached, hot-looking rock. She'd had her eye on the lapis lazuli earrings, but Molly thanked him.

Much later, when she and Pete fought at night, when she couldn't face another page of *Ulysses* or the smell of the French-English dictionary, she sometimes looked at the Gawain book and sometimes felt affirmed.

*

Pete preferred to work outside in summer, definitely not in retail. He filled boats with gas at the marina and hauled crap around the shipyard. On weekends he sometimes filled in at the lobster pound, unloading, on a good day, catch after catch.

For a few weeks he built sets for the Bay Harbor Dinner Theatre, spelled that way to make it fancier. A dozen twirlies without better offers worked there. Why not? Three months out of the city. Room and board, right on the water. Quaint little shops in the harbor.

Pete didn't say much, but Molly could tell he liked it, being close to loud, flirty people from away. He went to the cast house, a barn on the East Side that leaked. Once, he picked her up at the bend just past her parents' house, where his headlights wouldn't shine in. How good that had felt, walking along the road to Pete, little fireflies zapping around. *This is the very beginning*, Molly had thought.

"In the theater," someone said at the cast house party, after the water bong made its way around, "it's like your body is your work. You have to groom it all the time."

"What, like work out more?"

"Totally," said the dyed redhead. "It's a different way of existing. Rather than a shell that gets the self to the office or the lobster tank or wherever, where the self often drifts away and thinks of other things—"

"Like wishing for a ham and cheese sandwich while typing a memo or remembering a favorite pop song behind the cash register." This from a smirking blonde with a silver necklace that said Karla.

"Yes! Exactly. For most people those are just picture moments. Like snapshot moments. When you're in theater, you're have to be *engaged* in Being. All the time."

Molly realized she was the only one who wasn't stoned.

They were not grounded people, Molly decided. They risked coming across as false. They had trained themselves to be Capital Letter Names. Personalities. It was not something they could necessarily remove, like a uniform. It had to be developed, affected. With the worst of them you thought, *drop the act and just be real.* With the best it was hard to look away.

"Did you say lobster tank?" someone said.

"When? Oh. Lobster tank. Yeah."

"Lobster pound," said Molly, and Pete's face did something weird. "Lobster pound," she said again. "Pete works there sometimes."

"Cool," said Karla, after a while.

"And my uncles," said Molly. And then it was back to what made twirlies so fascinating and yet so tortured. Pete lifted his hand from Molly's thigh and spoke to the tall dancer from Philadelphia. Everyone else talked quickly, changing their minds. Molly thought of things to say, but then they moved on. She felt not pierced enough.

"You didn't have to correct them like that," said Pete, about to drop her off at the bend. "Lobster tank. Who cares?"

"What? It's called a 'pound.' What kind of asshole doesn't know that?"

"They're not assholes. They're just not lobstermen."

"Their faces change," said Molly. "It's weird. They change every second." She felt tight in her chest, trying to explain. "And you *work* there," she said.

"Just for a few weeks."

"No, I mean you work at the pound. You're embarrassed about it now?"

"You don't have to come next time."

They breathed in silence. "Walk me back," she said finally, though it wasn't very far. He paused, deciding if he would, flicking the tassle of the Dancing Bear air freshener. Then he closed the door without slamming it and stood close, taking her hand. It was too dark for Molly to see his face.

Pete's Mom, Mimi, invited her over for dinner before Pete had a chance to come up with an excuse. She made eggs and sausage, which Pete said they always had on Fridays. They listened to music, Nina Simone, and Molly was allowed to have wine. Pete smoked right in front of his mom and she emptied the ashtray when it was full. She forgot sometimes and spoke to Pete in French. Then she left them there alone as she took the dog for a very long walk. Pete took Molly to his room, which he'd decorated with European flags and carved wooden statues of animals. They had just enough time to put their clothes back on before they heard his mother sing out that she was home.

When Pete came to Molly's house for dinner, her father sat at the head of the table and spoke in long bursts. Pete could choose between water and milk and had to spray himself with Puma to cover up the cigarette smell. Molly's mother asked how his classes were going. When Pete talked about shop, she nodded and passed him more popovers.

"Good life skill, that," said her father.

On the porch, alone, Pete squeezed her boobs in the dark and kissed her on the neck. Then he hopped into his mother's car with the hood lined with pennies, just as the porch light came back on.

*

Molly took him to a party she'd been invited to, a nice house with a thick row of trees on either side and an assortment of guitars and amps plugged into a generator on the lawn. There was a keg of something warm, and pretty gauze curtains with new burn marks. Pete slouched at first, not speaking. Molly brought him a big red cup and then another until he understood he didn't have to be Frenchie here—no one knew what he was called the rest of the year because they'd all go away, come fall. Just like the twirlies. He talked a little to Caroline, a summer girl who worked with Molly at the new age store on Fridays, who wore a ski hat even though it was July. Her legs were tan and long.

Then he took Molly's hand in the dark and made the hand grab his crotch and said he wanted to be alone with her, but she wanted to talk to other people some more. The mosquitoes had bitten the fleshiest parts of her—thighs and upper arms. She scratched at the bites until they hurt. "I need a cup of ice," she said, but Pete didn't hear. His eyelids drooped, and his smile was stuck. "I can't wait to fuck you," he said, and Molly felt wicked, hearing it. He had the car keys, his mother's, and after one more they went to the car, parked close to a deep ditch. He maneuvered the road, the blackness of it stretching all along the Point.

But ahead there were lights. "Shit-fuck," he said. Molly found the gum. She unwrapped a piece for him first and thought about airplanes, how you were supposed to do the opposite—put the oxygen mask on yourself first and then worry about the person beside you. Or was that only if that person was a child? She tried not to chomp too much as Pete rolled down the window. She wondered what the officer would smell first, booze or mint.

And then they saw it, because Pete's headlights were still on, the arc of metal that had probably been a hood.

"Turn around," said the officer. His face said, *I didn't sign up for this.* Uncle of someone at school. "Turn around!" And they did, and the cars behind them would have to do the same. Pete and Molly were the first in line to see.

When the phone rang later it was Brenda from JV basketball. Her voice sounded like the radio, like a stranger Molly couldn't quite picture.

"It was Michelle in there," she said. There were three Michelles, so she said, "Michelle Sampson. They had to use the Jaws of Life."

In there. What an odd way to say it. "I know," said Molly. "We saw it first."

"Her boyfriend won't walk. We heard it on the CB."

"I have to go," said Molly.

The Guidance Counselor was on call. There was an assembly, and then another. There would be increased efforts to stop this kind of thing. Project Graduation. They'd take the seniors white water rafting or bowling in Portland. There would be painted Pringle cans by all the cash registers in town. Any bit would help. The senior yearbook would be dedicated to her.

Michelle's twin sister was back in school by then but she didn't have to go to the assembly.

In English they wrote about their feelings on wide ruled paper. *I'm so glad to have Pete in my life*, Molly wrote. She wondered if this was the right thing to say.

Insouciant, she thought, having recently aced that vocab test. An apt word for how Michelle had been. Like *The Outsiders*, boyish and hard. A sloucher. Her jeans were tight. She wore chains, a few of them, and thick mascara. She was how Molly would never be. There had been something nervy inside, pushing. The twin sister, who'd sat with Michelle at lunch, was nicer, a giggler. They'd both been in Molly's Math class, where Michelle sighed a lot, legs splayed. Where the sister dropped her pen and said *Oops*.

At the funeral Brenda was the only one who wore all black, plus a long onyx necklace from the new age store that Molly had worn behind the counter for one whole day. She remembered Brenda's voice on the phone, buzzed with excitement.

For a while Pete stopped taking beers out to Ocean Point. They used the bong instead. He was a good driver. He said it again. And soon the distant worry became a thrill, a dare. The roads were tricky, all those angles along the winding coast. Of course there were crashes. Of course it wouldn't be them. They were rushing down dark, back roads together.

On graduation day Molly and Pete took pictures with each other's parents. They were given a choice between the Chem-Free night and their own camping plans. Their parents wrote them notes. Molly unzipped the tent flap just in time for Pete to throw up by a tree.

"I should borrow your study habits," Michelle's twin sister wrote in Molly's yearbook. She signed it with a peace sign under her picture and her future plans: Dental Hygienist and lifelong happiness. Her quote was from an Air Supply song that Molly had considered too.

5

THEN NOTHING HAPPENED FOR quite a while.

They thought they saw a penguin at the tip of Ocean Point on a calm, gray day in January. It seemed arctic even before they saw the bird, with the sun a far away smudge they could look at without squinting. Molly wrote about the bird in her diary.

"Holy," she said at the time. The bird was knee-high, twisting its black head around to look at the road and the boarded-up summer houses. They watched it until Molly couldn't feel her fingers too well. They climbed back in Pete's truck to warm up.

"Do you think he's hurt?" she said. "I wish we had a camera." There were little piles of stones someone had made, *cairns*, she remembered, built to balance just so like the markers on Monhegan's trails, arrows that were easy to miss.

"He seems fine," said Pete. His presence loosened something in creatures. They plodded willingly toward him—dogs, cats, a small tortoise on Dover Road once. At the Common Ground Fair, the pigs found him in a whole row of reached-out hands.

No one believed them about the penguin, not even Pete's Mom. "A puffin, you mean."

"No, not a puffin," said Molly.

It was an auk, said Molly's father. Penguins didn't come to Maine, but auks did. It had to be an auk.

Maybe they'd see it again, said Pete. Sometimes they blasted the heat and undressed, and sometimes they just sat there and listened to BLM and waited. It wasn't an awkward kind of sitting, with the radio on and the sea churning at the window. Pete took Polaroids of a dead squirrel in the road and a tidal pool that was frozen. The sun cut through and made beams on the black water. When the sun looked streaky like that, pinpointing places below, Molly thought of God. Or she could believe that God existed. But then he seemed to forget about them.

She told Pete about it. Maybe she thought this way because of the Sunday mornings with the Methodists in the pew beside her father, her mother at the window seat reading mysteries at home. Because of the hymns, because of "Brightly Beams" in particular.

She could see Pete considering, taking it in, this private thing she'd let him have. He didn't laugh at her or argue about it. He said he only saw shadows and light.

When they did undress, she couldn't stop looking at him. How lean he was—his cheekbones, his bony ass. She wanted to remember this, how lovely he looked at Ocean Point with the sea sounds outside.

"Why are your eyes always open?" he asked.

"You look nice," she'd said. *Pretty*, she meant. *Pretty don't make porridge*, her father liked to say. But he was so pretty.

What if she was blind? She wondered if she'd feel the same. Deaf or blind? It was a question from a book she had. *The Book of Questions*. They left it in Pete's Mom's car and the questions were conversation starters when the songs on BLM were bad.

If she couldn't see him, would she feel the same?

Deaf, she told him. I'd pick deaf.

So would he, of course.

They drank and dumped the bottles in the hospital fundraising bin.

*

There was college. Pete didn't apply, and Molly's parents said she didn't have to go but maybe she should give it a try. Now that she'd waited a year to decide.

She'd thought it would be nice to finally have her own small room, a brown upholstered single in a dorm facing Baxter Boulevard. But she was blocked in by adjacent freshmen, or frosh, as they were supposed to say, which made them sound like amphibians. Her hallmates didn't always go to the classes that someone else paid for. They put stickers on their doors that would leave behind smudges. It was like going over to a friend's house when she was little. The smoky rooms, the unfamiliar toys. How unsettling to be surrounded by smells that weren't her own.

In the evening the hall was quiet. To save money, and to avoid the frosh, Molly used the tiny hall kitchen to prepare her potatoes and beans.

Molly and Pete were on a break, like Ross and Rachel, which meant they'd get married and have sex again when she returned to Bay Harbor.

It was Molly's idea. She remembered Career Day, their first time, sneaking out of school to be in her parents' bedroom alone, and didn't want Pete to be the only one.

It would be good for them, a mature thing to do. They wouldn't have to reveal too many details.

Pete hadn't taken much persuading.

Molly called Flip right after orientation.

6

FLIP PICKED MOLLY UP in Portland and drove her to the beach, the back seat of his Honda Civic stashed with moldy, chlorinated towels. Now that he was U. Maine Orono Swim Captain, he had to practice five days a week, he told her.

It was September, right after the tourists had gone. They shared a bottle of fizzy Poland Spring—no booze during the swim season—and stayed in the car. He balled up a towel and pressed it sweetly between Molly's head and the door handle, the only car left in the sandy lot. That earthy, chemical smell—Flip's broad, acned shoulders. His face was earnest, focused, eyes closed, counting his strokes. Molly was thinking of that gay Olympic diver—and then Flip's face crumbled sweetly into itself. He let his weight fall on her and she watched the lighthouse beam from Ram's Island begin to sweep across the goggles on the floor, two egg-shaped emeralds, and then they were in darkness again.

The next day she told him what she'd written about him on the wall of the little play-shed her father had built, how she liked the look of his butt in Speedos.

The guilty stab wasn't nearly as sharp as she'd expected.

When Flip's team qualified for All Eastern, there was a picture of his near-naked self in goggles, blue this time, on page one of the *Tribune*. Her father forwarded the paper and Molly studied the V of Flip's chest in her room, her hand busy under the blanket. She was not yet engaged, she thought, and taped the article into her journal. Here was a boy who could be taught to dress properly, a boy who was larger. She wanted to dance with him again, like she had in junior high at the Y. She wanted pictures where they looked well matched.

Flip's team lost at All Eastern, and then he failed too many classes. He joined the Army. They sent him to Arizona, Maryland, Korea, and Hawaii, the *Tribune* reporting each move. In his uniform he looked meaner, just like the other Bay Harbor boys in their basic training pictures.

*

Pete sent Molly a package for her twentieth birthday, thick with bubble wrap. She sat on her shit-brown carpet and turned up the radio to block out the shouting frosh. She peeled the tape off slowly.

"When's our break over?" said the card.

Inside was a miniature in oil, a tiny red dory with sunlight streaking down like fingers, like God.

She switched her major to Business. She got her Associate's and went back to Pete after two years instead of four.

7

IN BAY HARBOR, THE town Molly had known forever, it was possible to make the days matter less. It was possible for things to soften in the musty pull of sheets with naked Pete at night.

Molly had often been cold in their old Townsend house back then, too cold to sleep. There was a draft somewhere—she'd have to find it. Maybe the bay window, the boards underneath, leaking in ocean air. She tried to sleep but her legs twitched, her nose felt icy.

"It's so cold," she said.

"Tiny Tim," he said, and pulled her into the chest space made for her, her head there. She tried to believe this: She was Tiny Tim, someone who could be scooped up, and Pete was the one meant to do it. She had delicate limbs that could snap. She could curve into the arc of him and be warm.

In the morning her neck hurt. She would have to knead it, get out the cracks. She went to the pantry to do this, surrounded by cans.

"What are you doing?" he said, peering into the pantry, smiling at her.

"I'm doing yoga," she said, which they both knew was ridiculous. They weren't those kind of people.

He touched her bottom lip. "When I wake up and don't see

you there—I never know if it's because you're angry or because I'm snoring or because you're cold."

"I was cold," she said. *Such a pretty man.*

"And you could lie, say it's the snoring when it's really because you're mad."

"I'm not mad," she said, and they went back to bed until noon.

It was Sunday. *Fucked three ways to Sunday*, she thought. It was so very simple—he was calmer with sex. It couldn't possibly be that easy, but it seemed to be.

"What?" said Pete. It was noon but he reached for her thigh in bed again and tugged.

Was it three ways? Was that the expression? Maybe it was seven. That would be a busy day of rest. She felt swollen everywhere, full of him. She had to remember to take her pill. "We missed church."

But his limbs—the length of him. Cheekbones sharp. She shifted to check the clock—2:00 PM!—and he pulled her back. She had to melt again, pretend not to be in the day. She liked his limbs but she didn't want to miss out on the day.

"I'll get tea," she said.

She went to the pantry not to stretch but to finish it sometimes, her insides already squishy with him.

*

When Molly came back, Pete's paintings were up all over town. There were seaside views on the walls of Cutting Edge and the Black Orchid, the Italian place. And, most recently, in a small gallery on Back Narrows that belonged to a Floridian. The vaginas were there. Not subtle ones, not like Georgia O'Keeffe's. And some of them actually sold.

There had been several weeks of letters to the *Bar Harbor Tribune*, though the guestbook cited only five gallery visitors in three months.

"No," said Pete, when Molly asked him to write a letter back.

"Just one."

"There's nothing to defend."

"But it's not your crotch that's on display!"

It wasn't hers either, not literally, but everyone assumed it was. He'd asked her to model over spring break but she hadn't. Not like that, not in broad daylight where the neighbors could wave at them from across the bay.

Was she a prude? She wondered. If they were wicked stoned would she let him then, her skirt hiked up, her legs spread?

He'd looked at books instead. There was a gap in Molly's bookshelf where *Our Bodies, Ourselves* had been.

But she was impressed by him again—the steady lines, all that concentration. He worked outside on the rocks and she wanted to watch him, to see how it happened.

When he asked again, she modeled. She went through pop song lyrics and hymns, the poems from Ms. Patrick's class. The limericks her father had taught her. ("*A beautiful bird is the pelican. Its beak can hold more than its belly can.*") States and capitals. How many states began with M? She thought of movies with Kevin Bacon and bands with animal names. (Dinosaur Jr.? Did that count?) The first and last names of her teachers since kindergarten. Elements in the periodic table, but she could only remember five.

It was supposed to be sexy, wasn't it? It was supposed to be an excuse for rolling around. But Pete couldn't be distracted. He was sipping from a can, looking at her as though she was a jigsaw, an equation.

The pain in her back felt like a hook slicing through.

"I have to pee," she said, and through the bathroom window she watched him stretch. The air outside was damp with low tide and his shirt was unbuttoned, flapping. She could slide a hand there and start it herself.

Instead she looked at the painting, which was ugly and large. Greens and yellows where browns and blues should have been.

"You don't like it," he said.

"No."

"You don't find it flattering."

"But it's not about that, is it. It's about how you see me."

He paused. "This isn't how I see you."

"No? Not with green hair?"

"Not with green hair." He shifted.

"Let's do something we haven't done before," she said. "Like fuck on the rocks."

"Nice."

"Fuck on the rocks. What's wrong with that? I want to fuck you on the rocks."

He laughed. "It's wet on the rocks. It's just weird to hear you say it. We'd need a blanket."

He was so slender, she thought, so small. She could crush him if she wanted. His jeans hung low on his waist.

"So get a blanket," she said.

But instead he opened a new can. She returned to her pose.

A painter had to break down the world into small parts and study them. So what if it didn't make him horny. It would be nice to be able to capture things, Molly thought, staring at her husband staring at her. Good to have that skill.

8

"CAREFUL ONCE THE BABY'S born," the Lamaze teacher said. She was also the Town Clerk. "It's easy to let yourself go." She wore orange leggings and a tight Lycra top, as though they were about to do aerobics. They were in the same gym Molly had played basketball in, where Pete and the Twirlie had appeared in *Pippin.*

Let yourself go. Wasn't that supposed to be a good thing? On a rodeo bull with a lasso or standing up in the back of a convertible or parasailing above waves that looked like a cartoon color, aqua or turquoise.

Pete wouldn't care, she thought. He liked her large. He'd want her to keep feeling solid and real.

But she wondered if there was such a thing as too solid. If she'd eventually become a boulder.

At Ebbtide she ordered French fries and peanut butter on white toast. She had cravings lately too for "Jewish foods," as her father called them, bagels and chicken soup, coconut macaroons and potato pancakes, which you could get frozen at Shop N Save, but only in the summer. Foods that filled you at once and didn't have complicated, lasting tastes. Unlike garlic, which lingered for hours, reminding her. She wanted to have her food and be done with it, move on to the next meal.

When Emmett came, kids' foods were best: Cheerios and boxes

of raisins and applesauce. The little bottles of mashed peas and squash. "He goes though a lot of these, don't he?" said the cashier. Streaky blonde in her graying hair. Five years ahead of Molly in school.

She sometimes went to Shop N Save when she didn't really need anything, just to watch the girls behind the deli counter, legs like stumps supporting all that girth. She was nowhere near their size.

And to be a slip of a thing wasn't a compliment. And she came from a long line of hefty builds. "Husky," said Molly's mother. Husky was better. Husky was the dog the neighbors had, wolf-like, howling and bold on a long lead.

But next to Pete with his cheekbones, what did people think? The tiny ass, the skinny legs. And yet he had a surprising strength, a steely kind of will when he wanted to summon it. Wiry. He could press against her in a wild way and their strengths somehow matched.

She wanted to bring him more to eat, mornings—trays of waffles, mugs of sugary tea. She wanted to keep him breathing quietly beside her without having to do all that rolling around anymore.

Emmett learned to sleep at odd hours, and Molly watched repeats of *Murder She Wrote.* She realized how widespread the perception was—Mainers as quiet, simple types. *Taciturn.* It wasn't just a matter of being shy. It was a deliberate holding back by Angela Lansbury because too much nonsense could spoil things.

When Emmett turned one, Pete gave him a stuffed penguin.

"Hard to find," he said to Molly. "'Cause it's *not a puffin.*"

"It's not," said Molly. She kissed them both, her two pretty boys.

9

MOLLY LEARNED TO INTERPRET the silences early on from her uncles and cousins, her male coaches and teachers. But it's getting harder to measure the gaps with Pete. Aren't the French supposed to talk too much, too fast? So many words inside they need their hands to speak too? Maybe the longer you stay in Maine the less you feel like speaking, no matter where your people come from.

"What's wrong?" But he won't tell her. Which makes Molly feel like her sisters are right. She's too prickly, everything sticking to her too much.

She learns not to ask, not to discuss the things that felt heaviest. It makes Emmett wonder and cry. The too-hard scrubbing of a dish. A bite in her voice that doesn't match the words coming out.

She wonders how she caught it exactly, the habit of letting things stay packed down.

And Pete returns calm, smelling like Dentyne and sweat. He'd gone swimming in the Gut without her or sailing with a sculptor he'd met at the Thistle. You should see his library, his album collection, Pete says, then disappears to the basement before she can formulate further questions.

Without words it's easier to ignore something plain. Like the profile of the figure in the painting who looks just like the Twirlie.

Bad art is dishonest art, Pete read to her from a book once. He meant, in art he was allowed to be unkind.

*

For his birthday she gives him a cell phone. "For emergencies," she says. He knows what she means: For days when he decides to disappear.

Could she disappear too? A small upheaval would be useful. Nothing that would interest the *Tribune* but something they could recover from, like a sloppy kiss on the dance floor at Gray's.

She doesn't want him to have a suitable insanity anymore. She doesn't want to ever have to leave her pretty house by the sea.

Flip Johnson, she thinks, humping her in his car back then and probably thinking of his flip turns. That had been insane enough. That had been suitable.

So.

They keep pitting small rocks against each other. *Tap. Tap.* Marks left behind, dents that will make an eventual crack.

10

IN WINTER THE AIR inside is sharp with the woodstove smell—hot and dry—and Molly has to twirl a globule of Vaseline around each nostril with her pinky finger to keep from bleeding. She wants to sleep feeling chilly now, warmed just by skin and bones under red, wool blankets. But Pete throws on more logs instead, leaves the bedroom door gaping to let the heat in. He turns up the thermostat. Molly wakes up sweating, her nightgown twisted, her socks flung off and missing. She makes up reasons to get outside as soon as possible—wood for the small inside pile, just a piece or two more. Refill the birdfeeder. She puts on her boots and her coat only and the ocean cold blows up her nightgown, a lovely shot of air. It's good to get air down there. Otherwise you're never free of close cotton to your crotch. Molly worries about her crotch this way. Someone has to.

Until the cold from the harbor begins to sting.

She's ready to face the lists then, the diaries: one for birthdays and anniversaries and when to mail the appropriate cards; one for household things such as library due dates, dentist appointments, prescription refills, weekly dinners with her parents; one for herself, which doesn't have a lot of space. Small rectangles, two fingers wide. *What if we'd met in the summer?* she writes. *One of us from away. Parties. Wine coolers. Summer jobs. Gone in the fall.*

Sandy and Danny kind of thing. But I guess they got back together too.

She keeps it in the pail of rock salt, a place where Pete isn't likely to dig. Still, she uses a code. Bad sex is BS. Horny dreams of Flip are HDOF. Worries about Pete are HT, husband trouble. Emmett concerns, ET.

There is another journal for Emmett's mementos. First word, first haircut, first steps, first independent bowel movement, favorite stuffed animal and book. (Peter Rabbit; *The Grinch*). The first time he collected shells at Ocean Point.

Pete says he keeps everything important in his head. He has a remarkable memory for names and places, phone numbers and dates. Photographic, Molly told people at a Christmas party, once.

Not really, said Pete.

Anyway, she's brave today, having risen before her husband and son. The house is quiet, and she has choices: read, walk, do dishes. She should do dishes. If she doesn't do them now she won't want to do them later and he won't do them, and her breakfast will taste better if the sink is empty, that's a fact.

But reading—a whole chapter uninterrupted.

But the dishes.

And so the turn begins, and she hates him already, the warm one in there under all those old blankets, all his dead weight, the heat of his solid sleep—she has to do the dishes when she wants to read. He thinks her weekends are shapeless, unplanned, no pressure for her to go to the basement and create.

She leaves the dishes. She makes herself read with her feet on the couch. She pulls on her tangled hair. She doesn't get up to brush her teeth though her mouth tastes foul, and she doesn't get up to take her vitamins and the dishes are dirty and when he opens the bedroom door (always with a jolt, the hinges complaining, the surly look of him making her madder, which makes him madder) she wants to rip the sleep from him then because he hates day. He'd read to her once, something about the land of the midnight sun—how awful it would be. Naked in hot springs and not-yet-dark, all the fucking time.

She's not a reader, but a lazy, messy wife in her sweatpants who hasn't yet brushed her teeth.

She says something about the dishes, and he says something about having plowed out the driveway. When's the last time you took out the garbage, he says.

A few days ago, when it was full.

Right, he says.

Right. Emmett's calling for her now.

But sometimes, before Emmett wakes but after feeding the birds and filling in another journal square, she's ready to crawl back in. And sometimes he reaches back like he's been waiting. He's heavy with sleep but he knows it's his wife stroking him hard. She matches his breathing, and this doesn't feel strange. She wants to be tucked back in, smothered a little. She wants it to feel like high school again.

That is the only place for touching now, in their too-warm bed.

Nights it's the opposite, of course. She gets there first. When he comes to bed it's like grass ripping from the base of her brain, a pull from somewhere healthy to somewhere not. The bedroom smells like a liver processing booze, the sweet-sickly burning off. She has to turn away from him, get to cleaner air.

No one makes you do it, say her sisters. You don't have to do anything you don't want to do.

Who will do it, then? she says.

Once, when she came back from the salt rock pail, he was at the table, eyes closed, her U. Southern Maine coffee cup clamped to his ear.

"The Tahitian sea," he said. "I can hear it." He'd been reading the Symbolist book she gave him.

She resisted, clamping onto all her boiled up hardness.

But then, as though someone else was deciding for her, she pushed out a small smile. She made the hardest thing dissolve.

"I *can*," he said. "Listen!"

What if Emmett has it too? What if his cute oddities—repeated rhymes, attachment to raisins—are signs of future obsessions?

She should nip the fantastical things in the bud. Become the shrew. *No such thing as the Easter Bunny. Not a fairy, Em. That's a firefly.*

At the bank she doesn't sit down. She counts out twenties. She talks too long to Adam Pruitt about the likelihood of red tide.

She has to go outside to think at all. After work she picks up Emmett from his grandparents and drives to the Point, away from the stink of their living room.

When they fight, Pete says, *Don't run away*, even though he'd been the one to bolt. Twice. All the way to Old Orchard. And then his spontaneous daytrip to Monhegan, solo.

When he came back she didn't wanted to look at him. She didn't want to smile. She wanted to remember how mad she was so it wouldn't happen again.

But it took so much energy to stay that way.

She could have a bag packed, ready to go. Like going to the hospital.

Do laundry, she writes in the diary. *Buy milk*. She can't remember if she refilled the birdfeeder. Yes, she did, she sees, looking out the bay window, but she can't remember doing it, her body and mind split from their tasks.

"Disturbing, your memory," says Pete.

Wouldn't it be tiring to remember every motion? Where would she store it all? She's running out of room. She needs more space for her days.

*

When they fight she stays in the guest room. She wants something else in her brain, something that will push out the shit and bloom into goodness. A puzzle to unravel that isn't connected to her. She pulls *Ulysses* from the small, dusty shelf and turns again to the end.

If she ever has to teach grammar, she'll use *Ulysses*. She'll copy Molly Bloom's monologue and ask her students to punctuate. They'll have to guess where the pauses should go. Though someone has probably done this already.

When would she ever need to teach grammar?

There have to be Cliff Notes. Maybe at the library. Or maybe she'll just read it back to front.

In the morning she's there before him in the breakfast nook and doesn't look up. "Sleep well?" she says.

"Not really," Pete says. Icy.

She clears her throat. "I'm re-reading *Ulysses*."

"Oh. Re-reading. You mean *The Odyssey*." They'd read pieces of *The Odyssey* in Senior English. Or Molly had read them and explained them to Pete. She'd typed up his paper for him too.

"No," she says. "*Ulysses* by James Joyce."

He was quiet, stirring milk into his tea until a whirlpool formed. "It was banned," he says. "For being porn."

"It's not porn," she says. But she kind of hopes it is. And that breaks them both, saying porn out loud in the morning together. They crack back into their old selves without having to apologize.

She could be like Molly Bloom. Here's a Molly who says yes

to things, even when she shouldn't. And Pete could be more like Leopold, endlessly adoring, even when she cheats.

But what about the *having a* very *bad fight* option and just living in bitterness forever? Writing someone off completely? People do it all the time, not just on Jerry Springer. They decide to hate each other because it's easier, maybe, than trying to forgive. Done.

Except it can't be that easy—there must always be a deep niggle of anger directed at that person, a force that makes it hard to smile genuinely. It's what she thinks of when she hears the word "divorcee." Someone incapable of smiling genuinely.

Maybe not. Maybe it's as easy as shaking off a bad haircut, just pretending your ends aren't chopped. And eventually they won't be.

Molly has stopped getting haircuts at A Cut Above. Her hair is too long for her face. She tucks it behind her ears at the bank and waits.

11

THEN COMES THE NIGHT she locks the bathroom door and crouches in the dry, hairy bathtub. She feels like she's been running. Her husband knocks on the door, and she wonders if she can crawl out the bathroom window if she has to. No. She can see she won't be able to fit.

She unlocks the door. Why? She's afraid of what else he'll do, and there's some archaic brainwashing in her that tells her to obey. It isn't civilized to be hiding in the tub from him.

"Don't be so dramatic," he says, and holds her until she has to pull away. She sleeps in the guest room, trying to understand *Ulysses* again. Touching the spine of the French-English dictionary.

In the morning she leaves before he's up. She looks at her cell phone in the break room and has thirteen missed calls, seven voicemails, three texts. She lets Shirelle Johnson take too long at the kettle before pouring her own. She photocopies the memo slowly. She waits for the bathroom to be empty and applies her SPF 45 Chapstick in hard repetitive strokes.

Maybe he's hurt himself. Or someone else. Maybe he's calling from jail. But you're only allowed one call from jail, not thirteen. And she's pretty sure they don't let you text.

She snaps the stall door shut and sits down on the toilet to listen. *I don't want to be married to anyone else*. He loves her, he says. He's crying.

She doesn't listen to the other six messages. He picks up on the first ring and she says it back to him, easily.

Why? says her co-worker, Maureen, on a green tea break.

Because, says Molly, her chest unblocked for a moment, it's hard to resist a charming artist, even if he isn't charming most of the time. There's the hope that he will be cured of his faults one day, that the artistry will eventually smudge out and override the rest of it. As that Canadian, Margaret Atwood, wrote, in another book Molly kept in the guest room, inside the imperfect husband is a perfect husband maybe, just waiting to be lured out by Molly for good.

They have a date night.

"Date night?" her father says.

"Your father doesn't believe in dates once you're married," says her mother. "It must be a generational thing."

Her father grins at Emmett, who won't grin back. Molly's mother waves to Pete and Molly from the porch.

After shots at Gray's, Molly writes on a napkin, "*Colors. Sacrifice everything you have for them.*"

"Very nice," says Pete. "You read the Symbolist book too."

"That's what you want? The artist's life?" Is this her speaking? It doesn't feel like her.

"You're drunk."

"You and fucking Van Gogh."

"That wasn't Van Gogh," he says.

He's so smirky and calm. She wants to make him topple over.

"We're both messed up. That's why it works so well."

"I'm not messed up," she says. "Nothing works."

He smears a cold, skinny fry around his plate, trailing red without lifting it to his mouth. "What does that even mean?" he says.

"It means, it's not working. It's broken." People are looking at them, people they know.

"Wow," he says. "You're still pissed about Old Orchard."

In her blood is a kind of spark that makes her feel better. She gets up from the barstool, forgetting her purse.

"You're into pointing out the sin but not so into forgiving," he says. But his eyes look a little scared finally.

"Enjoy your burger," she says, though his burger is gone. Her head is no longer connected to her body and it's just what she wants.

She leaves Gray's. Leaves him with the bill and her purse, which she knows he'll eventually bring out to the car. He'll finish her burger and both their beers and he won't pick up his emergency cell phone. He'll pay. He'll chat up the waitress, a summer girl.

By the time he reaches the parking lot she has a new one for him. "You're the most arrogant cocksucker on the planet."

"Cunt," he says. Just to get her attention, he'll say later. *I'd give my left nut for you, in actual fact.*

Was that the damaged nut? she'll wonder. The one scarred from the bicycle accident? She won't be able to remember.

For now she runs away from the car.

She calls Harbor Taxi, "aptly singular," as her father says, and twenty minutes later it comes. Huey the driver played Judas in *Godspell* senior year. "I'll send you a check," she says.

"No worries," says Huey. "I know where you live."

At home, Molly claims the bedroom and shuts the door. She reaches for the pillow and pushes her face into it and wonders if it's possible to suffocate that way.

Eventually, Pete follows her. He takes the pillow away and holds her wrists down when she starts to swing at him. *Motherfucker,* she hears, the squeal of a crazy person, someone being attacked. Her own voice. "I'm not hurting you," he says. "We're going to work it out," he says, panting. "Tonight. This is going to be a rational, mutual decision."

She kicks at him, her husband, and he tries to hold onto her again. "*Don't fucking touch me, motherfucker.*"

It's good that she has these instincts still. Both flight and fight.

He lets go and she scrabbles away from him, knocking her knee against the bedpost.

He takes his car keys from the dresser then. "White trash," he says. "Townsends."

"Right." She laughs. "Unlike the Gerards of Lewiston."

Who else can hear them? The windows open, their voices bouncing on the water. A light comes on from the house across the bay. Maybe she'll hear a siren. Who would it be? Officer Roy? She could dismiss the charges. Would they print it in the *Tribune* anyway?

But no one comes. No one is ever coming to catch them.

He sleeps in his truck.

At dawn he comes back in.

"You can't go," he says.

I didn't go! She feels the welling up of very dark things, familiar, and she cries and can't help it and his arms are wrapped around her, his face pressed to her neck and he says, "Fuck. You're crying."

"Because it's scary," she says. Maybe this is what she's addicted to—the peaceful, easy feeling after the shit show. The relief of contact after ripping everything to bits.

"It is scary," he says. "We have to work it out."

But she means, *No, it's scary that we act like beasts and now we're pretending everything's fine.*

"Thank god Emmett's not here," he says.

She wants Emmett there. He keeps them safer.

She has to get ready for Saturday hours but he won't stop his squeezing.

Molly wears a lot of make up. There's a throb in her knee. Her thumb hurts from something. She buys a large coffee at the Irving station and gets to her window ten minutes late.

None of this makes her life more interesting.

She could go back to school. That would be interesting.

"You look nice," says her boss.

"A little tired today."

"Me too. Watch the Sox game?"

Defeated, she looks better? She can feel it on her break walking downtown. The young cashier at the bakery, suddenly intrigued by this person he sees every day. The postal carrier, waving. They can smell it on her maybe, the smallness. Her eyes glassier. Such a big, pretty girl but still she needs care.

She remembers you aren't supposed to go swimming near sharks or camping near bears while you have your period. They can smell the blood.

All day she keeps shitting and shitting—bad liquid coming out of her at last.

"Sorry, bad burger," she says at work.

Maureen, at the sink, makes a face and agrees.

She picks up Emmett at her parents' as planned. "How was date night?" asks her Dad.

She buckles in her son and gets it, at last. *I'll have to be the one to go.*

12

AT THE DRUGSTORE, FLIP Webber chooses an Ace bandage and a pack of Fisherman's Friends. He has a small scar above his eyebrow that looks like a checkmark. His nose is bigger—bad flip turn? By the time she walks the aisle she sees him swimming into the pocked wall of the Y pool, the pink seeping into the white stripe of his weathered Speedos.

"Hey! Pretty lady!" he says. He reaches out to hug her and smells clean, like hay and Old Spice. He says her old name, and she doesn't correct him. Neither one of them look at her ring.

They'd still look good together in pictures, she thinks. His hair is longer and his eyes are not as excited.

"What's new?" He grabs onto the shelf with his free hand and she wonders if he'll swing himself down aisle that way, a jungle gym trick, testing his triceps. They're next to the hydrogen peroxide, and Molly needs a bottle. It's why she came down the aisle. She doesn't reach for one.

What can she tell him? *Pete took your place after college. Because he seemed like a soulful boy at first and because he'd been watching me since fifth grade. Everyone else called him Frenchie but he didn't seem to care what people thought and I liked that about him too. He wrote poems and painted. He had pretty eyes and lips like a girl. He was small but solid and when we had sex for the first time it wasn't in a car, but in a real bed, my parents' bed in fact, and he cried. I made him wait until Career Day—remember that? The day of no classes, just people coming in to talk about being a realtor or a travel agent. No Rockettes or broadcast journalists. I figured I didn't need to go to Career Day. I'd just keep going to Art Club because I wanted to be an Art Teacher then—it was my favorite class. You didn't necessarily have to be good at art to be in Art Club. And Pete was there.*

On Career Day my parents were at work. We listened to Prince. The room was very bright and the sun made it harsh, and after I felt a burning there, a chafing, but also a rush. It was impossible not to tell anyone, like the day you finally get your license. I saw Julie by my locker and before I said anything she said, You look different. I can tell.

I have a new career, *I said, and we still laugh about that sometimes.*

*Later there were lake sounds and mosquito bites—Skin so Soft not working, legs wrapped around each other on a picnic table. I had a curfew, and we always just made it. He liked to tuck his head into my neck and bite me a little. "*Zee fe-male haz to be happy,*" he said, putting it on. "*Zis is zee most important thing.*" Then he said the same thing in French, to impress me.*

For months we had sex every day after school—in a tent he put up in the woods when the mosquitoes got too bad. The sex made me feel related to him, linked by fluids. It's hard to explain but I felt pulled—it wasn't an unpleasant feeling. Away from him I felt not quite right, like I'd left my wallet somewhere.

I worried sometimes that other girls would catch on. There was only one other who noticed him, though. We don't ever talk about it.

"Not so much," says Molly to Flip. "Emmett just turned four."

"My word," says Flip. "And how old's your son?"

"That's my son, Emmett." Our son.

"Oh!" he laughs. "I was thinking it was a pet's name. Hey—do you run?"

She looks at her feet. Bean boots with wool socks. "Not so

much," she says.

"I'm doing the 10K in the fall. Signed up yesterday. Want to sponsor me?" It's kind of a high, he tells Molly—running until your body has no more fuel but to turn in on itself. Eating itself up. "Remember the Codfish Race?"

Yes, the Codfish Race. In full foul-weather gear, hugging the fish to his chest—a cod the size of a small pig. The Student Council nominated the fastest—at first they picked Pete as a joke, the class pothead.

"Imagine if Frenchie *had* done it," he says now, laughing.

"Peter," says Molly, correcting him. She picks up the bottle of hydrogen peroxide.

Soon after the Codfish Race, she remembered, Flip had discovered pot too. Another way the brain could turn in on itself.

Pete still liked to remind her of this, how Flip had become the pothead for a while. She doesn't say so in the aisle of Rite Aid.

She thinks of the photo in her journal, which is why she says, "Still swimming?" She's conscious of her own torso, which is not at all a V.

Flip doesn't answer. He reaches out to take the bottle from her hand and puts it back on the shelf. He takes the hand without the ring and she feels a warmth rise up and knows what will happen next.

It would have been apt to return to Ocean Point, but it's high summer, the middle of the day. And they're too old to do it in a car. Instead Molly follows him to his room at the Flagship Motel and it happens quickly on top of the anchor-patterned bedspread, and then once more, slowly, in the bathroom, Flip hitching up her sundress to watch her from behind in the mirror.

"Call me tomorrow?" he says.

"Here? Why are you staying here?"

"You have room in the shed?"

"Might be awkward."

"It would only be temporary."

He kisses her again. She nods and pulls down her dress. She lets the door click softly behind.

At the house Emmett has trampled a banana into the throw rug and Pete hasn't noticed.

"You look like you got some sun," he says.

"It's gorgeous out," she says, busying herself with the squashed, yellow pulp.

"You seem chipper," he says as she clears the plates and glasses.

"I shouldn't be?" she says. Things clatter in the sink in her hands without breaking.

"You should be," he says.

In the bathroom she crouches and cries until Emmett calls for her to come and find his Elmo book right now, please.

13

Flip has an insanity, she learns—a common one. He likes the Patriots. He watches all the games at the Thistle, and this is how Pete ran into him there on a Sunday afternoon.

Molly knows Pete couldn't give two shits about the Patriots. He'd gone for a pint of Belhaven. Or four.

"Frenchie!" Flip called him, and then sang the song by Steve Perry. Or so Pete was quick to tell her when he got home.

She'd smiled at Flip at the finish line in a way that meant, What are we doing here in this godforsaken town where they make you do this with a giant cod? *After that he had the courage to ask her to dance to a Journey song at the Y. He gripped her palm after, making sweat suction them together a little. She didn't want to get away to speak to her girlfriends or buy a Twix from the vending machine or call her mother to say where she was and how much longer she'd be there.*

Pete hadn't been there that night. Or maybe he'd came and gone, preferring to hang out with Campbell the Stoner in the parking lot.

When she can't get away to meet Flip she takes a jar of Skippy's out to the rocks and licks slowly, losing track of how many spoonfuls. The Twirlie is back. And so they're even again.

14

"I HAVE TO GET back to the island," Pete says for the second time, like he doesn't have a choice about it. His voice is clipped like C3P0, which makes Molly snort, which Pete mistakes as a snort about him leaving, about his needs and wants and talents.

"You should," she says. Last time she'd been stirring oatmeal for Emmett and hadn't bothered looking up at him, her husband. This time she looks.

Let me go, she sees. *Please, please let me go.* Are his eyes wet? Is he stoned? He's waiting for Molly to give permission. He wants to make this her fault too.

Molly's skin feels prickly, like she's sweating inside. *This is happening*. Something is actually breaking here.

"When are you coming back?" she says. It's been so long since they've asked proper, direct questions.

Her husband's boots are tied. His shirt is tucked. She can smell the shaving cream, fake limes. He'd trimmed his sideburns and the patch where his cheeks met his beard. The bubble-wrapped easel rests against the basement door behind him.

"Please tell Emmett," he says.

She wills her heart to shut the fuck up and it does, just long enough for something steely and beautiful to rise up to her throat. "You're a real shit," she says. She turns to finish the dishes, and he doesn't wait for her to recover. He slams the door. He starts the truck.

From above she hears Emmett's voice—"Mumma!"—and she wakes then, running out in her rubber gloves to fix it.

Pete fiddles with the lighter in his lap.

"Will you return?" she shouts. "Today?"

But her husband's lips are set. He won't roll down the window. He turns one more time to look at her. *I have to*, his face says. *I don't hate you but I have to.* Then he steers expertly around the potholes and is gone.

Emmett stands on the front step, the leg of his stuffed Big Bird smeared with toothpaste. He yawns at the rattle and dust of the truck and asks his mother for breakfast. "The water," he says, meaning the sink of dirty dishes filling up.

"I know," says Molly. She lifts her son and smells him, sour hair and mint.

"Ow," he says. "Tight." She puts him down and lets him run.

Molly's mind is too tired to loop through it anymore, but still it keeps looping.

I have to get back to the island.

Daytrip. It could be. It could be.

But it's dark out. The ferry has been back since four.

Shit. Had she said that? *You're a real shit.*

She puts Emmett to bed, smokes a forgotten roach from Pete's ashtray, and walks out to the rocks. She wouldn't appear to be waiting, she thinks, if someone were to see her. Who would see her? The stars are cutting through, white-yellow, tons of them—she can see them as 3D, not as a sheet of stars above but as pocks of light, some closer and some further away. She used to be able to see this without the pot, but not anymore. She remembers the constellation chart her father had cut from the Cheerios box.

Some of the biggest, brightest stars might be furthest away, he'd told her, and some of them may have died a long time ago—it just took awhile before the way they really looked traveled to earth. It was a tricky idea for Molly to swallow. How could the light die before it even got there? Like that phrase they shouldn't say anymore, Indian giver. What they were seeing was something that didn't exist at all anymore.

Around her the trees are black—anything could be hiding there. Her husband, for instance.

If he comes back again will she pretend, again, that she doesn't have questions? Is he waiting for her to ask?

The sea rushes and pushes. She could stay there, get a blanket and keep watching the stars and when he comes back to her maybe he'll panic, wonder where she is, think maybe she's drowned herself with rocks in her pockets. She'll hide in the woods and watch him cry on the rocks with Emmett, see his pushed-down self come spilling out at last.

Until then, she'll take down the paintings. There aren't many. The still life with clams. The miniature above the toilet, an abstract—a dory against electric blue. Ten different kinds of blue for sky and water and shades of air in between. Her birthday gift, the blotchy rays of yellow slicing through. She can't remember telling him that, though she must have—how the sun looks like God when it sifts through that way.

Emmett will notice the blank spaces. She'll have to come up with a reason why.

Or maybe Emmett won't ask. Like his father didn't ask. The Neruda poems she'd hid last year, an old Valentine's Day present from Pete. A hole in the shelf and he said nothing for weeks.

But then he did. "Why? To mess with me?"

She was falling inside from a great height, ready to say why, maybe. "I just—did it," she said.

Give me more, his face said.

"It's just not something that's true anymore, is it?"

His face was rigid but the answer seemed to satisfy him. He left her alone and went to the Thistle.

A month passes. Molly's mother comes with paper towels and Lysol. Her sisters bring books and CDs (*Codependent No More*; *How Stella Got Her Groove Back*; *Jagged Little Pill*). The deli guy gives her half a pound of boiled ham for free. Someone leaves a dish of lasagna in her car. The plumber comes, after months of not coming. Her cousins refill the driveway without having to be told. They send a bill but say she can pay whenever.

Molly watches old episodes of *Friends* with her father, glad to hear his easy laugh in her living room. He throws his head back and the sound comes peeling out like a high-pitched cough or the beginning of a sneeze. There are plenty of amusing things left to consider, her father means.

Grammy had laughed like that, an unfiltered kind of cackle, as Molly sat on a stool beside her. She cut potatoes with the knife pointing toward her wrist, which Molly should never do herself. Grammy's fingers had ruts from cutting hard things the wrong way for decades.

"Remember Grammy's fingers?" she says to her father during the commercial.

"Tough," he says.

"You laugh like her," she says. She sips some more of her tasteless tea, wanting a Mojito.

Laughter will make Molly less likely to sink. She will not sink. Sinking would make it impossible to deal with Emmett, hard to push back the Pier One coverlet and face more Cheerios.

"I like that Rachel," says her father, but he doesn't know what she sees in Schwimmer.

Molly likes Chandler, who does everything Monica tells him to do.

She decides she doesn't need her sisters' books. She understood that Pete's insides solidified long ago, that it wasn't really her fault. It's as though she married the giant cockroach man in *Men in Black*. On the outside he seemed relatively normal—an occasional limp, a waft of sulfur—nothing too extraterrestrial. But inside, all along, he'd been oozing with alien cockroach parts.

Emmett's insides don't have to be the same.

If people ask outright, she'll say Pete took too much Oxy, which he had sometimes. It made his brain not quite right, permanently.

"Let him be," her father says of Molly's long, worried face. Her father doesn't say, *You're better off without him* or, *You'll find someone else*. But she likes to think this is part of his meaning too.

Is she supposed to take the ferry out, talk Pete out of it? Is she supposed to try to live on Monhegan for a time? The islanders might remember that Townsends had owned things there long ago. Would she have to spend a winter there? How nuts would it make a person? Emmett would get fed up and get in trouble and eventually have romances with prep school girls in summer houses. He'd try lobstering and find it cold and dull. He'd learn to hate the day-trippers.

She remembers the boat ride to Monhegan with Pete for their anniversary, water shining as the ferry pushed through. Molly had looked hard (they'd sipped Shipyard Ale, although it was only ten o'clock) and the water was gray and white. How was that possible? Such a bright blue and yellow day, and the water was steely. For a moment she was able to see all the colors as they actually were, instead of how she thought they should be. The sun made little white lines jerk and shine on the surface. It wasn't a relief to see this. It was like trying to explain why a joke was funny. Or learning all the lyrics to a song she loved. (That time she bought *Under the Cherry Moon* at Bull Moose Music—how disturbing some of the words were, words she hadn't caught or hadn't bothered to catch. She didn't want to know.)

She'd thought Pete would paint on Monhegan then, but he didn't want to be another artist there. He laughed at them in their stupid hats.

A painter had to do it all the time—rip through all the fluff and take a real, long look. How tiring not to give in to blue on occasion. To have to diligently record all that gray and white.

But when he got it right—how satisfying that must be. A flash of seeing the true shades.

Or maybe people like Pete didn't have to break things down so explicitly. Maybe they could rely on intuition. They knew how to feed the impulse to their hands. That was the most remarkable thing about it to Molly—to see the world that way and then make the body translate—the hands moving along blank space.

Because Pete could do this, she didn't have to.

She wondered, then, what it was she had to do.

They docked and climbed the hill to the island graveyard, which wasn't as creepy as Molly had hoped. The Earth, Wind and Fire song blew into her brain and wouldn't disappear. *It's written in the stone.* Could they live out there? So little chance of rescue, on an island.

She dragged Pete to his ancestor's house on the beach, though he didn't seem to care. She hadn't thought to bring a camera. The ferry ride back took forever and Emmett hadn't even known they were gone. He hadn't wanted to leave his grandparents' house, where, after the trip to Story Land, he could sit in a wading pool all afternoon, clapping with Molly's joyous pot-bellied father.

"It's a lucky year," Molly's mother says out of nowhere, shutting and opening cabinets in the next room. "Your luck is going to change. I feel it."

Stop it with the paper towels, Molly doesn't say. *No one's painting here.*

But she knows her mother believes in luck—both good and bad and the superstitions that cause them. There are specific rituals for Christmas—the dreadful, loping sign her sister Megan had hammered out (Merry X-Mas—not enough room for the Christ). Placed on the mantel to ensure a festive season. Fortune cookies had to be consumed or the fortune wouldn't matter.

"Shh," says her father. "Ross's monkey got loose."

Her mother isn't so quirky. It's common knowledge that the fortune cookie has to be eaten. Even Flip knows this, as he'd demonstrated once at China By the Sea.

Maybe she can still be an artist. "It was Art Club," Molly says to her parents. "What if I'd never joined Art Club?"

"Sweetie," says her mother.

"You loved Art Club," says her father.

I loved Pete. Or the idea of him. I thought he was something I could study.

"Gifted," she says. "I wasn't gifted."

You are," says her mother. "You're talented and gifted."

"My assemblages sucked," says Molly.

Her father laughs again but it isn't at her.

I was a lousy apprentice.

"You make a wicked chili," says her mother. Then, "I hate that Schwimmer. He's always falling down."

15

HER SISTERS SUGGEST SMALL pets to fill the space, to make it louder. They drive Molly and Emmett to Petco in Cook's Corner and pick out goldfish. Emmett wants a gerbil and a parakeet too, and Molly says yes. He loves them for a month and then forgets.

Molly feeds them and worries about forgetting. She writes a note and puts it on the bathroom mirror. But on weekends she sees the note and then makes coffee first (not tea), stirs in sugar slowly, gets lost in the paper. The parakeet flies away when she tries to clean the cage. She finds it in on the driveway, frozen, and can't tell Emmett.

"He had to hibernate," she says. "Up and left us through the cat flap."

"Why?" says Emmett. "We've never had a cat."

"It's what birds do. It's not personal," she says. She reminds him about the gerbil and the fish.

Jekyll eats Heckle—or maybe it's the other way around. Heckle is the girl fish, Emmett says. Then Heckle eats her own children, sucks up the little snot-pile of eggs stuck to the side of the tank. And then she dies herself, floating there with her children digesting inside.

Molly flushes her down the toilet.

She remembers the awful crunch of caviar under her tongue. The crackers unfamiliar, not Ritz or Saltine, and the fishy taste made her want to eat a lot of ice cream. They'd been invited to the *Tribune* Christmas party—her father had made a small donation. Molly had thought the publisher must be nice because she put live bunnies in the windows of the *Tribune* office at Easter. But then she'd gone and served up baby fish on crackers.

The pleasure was in the texture, her mother said, when they could be themselves again in the car.

It was a novelty, said her father. It was about consuming something different—not the actual taste. Then her parents talked about the people at the party and Molly joined in and she would tell her sisters it had been divine. They'd missed it, stayed at home to watch the *Grinch* for the billionth time.

Should she get a bunny for Emmett?

No. When the gerbil dies, that will be it.

She finds lost toys kicked under Emmett's bed—tiny Yoda and Papa Smurf, passed down from Molly's collection. She buries the Ken doll in a small mound under the porch, orange pine needles sprinkled on top.

"Mumma?" Emmett asks, the dirty, naked doll in his hands.

Hibernation? She doesn't have the will to explain. She sees how anatomically incorrect Ken is and how confusing this must be, particularly for boys. She swipes Ken's privates with a dishtowel and tries to remember the jokes her father taught her as a girl, the limerick about the pelican and the made-up book called *The Yellow Stream*.

"By I.P. Freely!" she tells her son. But it isn't as funny to him.

For Emmett's Christmas concert Molly wears a sweater patterned with pine trees and her grandmother's pearls. She pulls her hair back with a scrimshaw barrette, takes Emmett to his classroom, mittens dangling and clasped to the sleeves of his coat, which he places on the hook with his name. Then her son sings "Up On A Rooftop" from the second row of kindergarteners as Molly sits on a folding chair and imagines humping the music teacher. Under the coat hooks, the smell of dirt and baby powder, a row of plastic lunchboxes tapping together above them: Dora, Barney, Sponge Bob.

This lumpy man with sweat stains, whose face she can't see from where she sits.

The music man? They'd say at the bank.

"Did you hear it, Mumma?" Emmett asks.

She nods. She can nod without it being a lie. After the music man, she'd thought about all the shaved, sweatered husbands in the front row.

She won't call Flip just yet.

Mornings, Molly opens the fridge and stares for a while, wonders if it would be wrong to start with Guinness. Guinness is good for you. Good, black iron in her blood.

She makes strong coffee and reads the *TV Guide*. She slips a hand inside the loose drawers of her flannel PJs.

Odd how the body adjusts and wakes itself, how the brain begins to feel connected even when it doesn't want to, just from light and caffeine and other stimuli pouring in. From the momentum of her steady, rubbing hand.

Odd how the body recovers before the mind.

She experiments with not drinking coffee. She leaves the burner on without the kettle, and it's Emmett who shows her. Red! he says, because the burner is almost that shade, his head inches from it. She starts drinking coffee again.

She makes banana bread from the mound of blackened fruit in her freezer. "I made banana bread," she announces at work.

"With chocolate chips." Maureen helps her finish the loaf before lunchtime. Chocolate smudges on the deposit slips.

She goes on the Reggae Cruise, which she hasn't done since before her wedding. There's a band now, and one reggae song out of every four—no one really wants three hours of reggae. They go to Bath and back, past the summer houses on Sprucewold and Southport, where too much sound carries still, Bad Company drifting in during cocktail hour. Summer people on white porches who only want to hear the sea.

Van Morrison, CSN, CCR, Steve Miller. A few Peter Framptons. Molly dances and stares at the receding harbor and talks to the people she's been talking to since kindergarten. A bachelor party takes up most of the upper deck, and the band makes the groom-to-be sing, "Feel Like Making Love." Back at the dock, half the boat piles into Gray's Pub.

But three hours is enough for Molly. It's about two hours too long.

The girls at the bank invite her to darts tourneys and bowling nights. She tries to sing "I Will Survive" at karaoke. She has to roll into the driveway carefully, making herself look cheery for her father, who says, "Good night out with the girls?"

"Wicked," she says.

"Why bother, then," he says. "If it isn't any fun?"

Because on Monday they'll ask too many questions. *Didn't see you at Gray's.*

And there's no use lying. It's too tiny a place.

16

MOLLY DRINKS THE LAST Guinness in the fridge and doesn't buy another six-pack.

She listens to Suzanne Vega and pours seltzer with lime and reads about artist colonies in the thick and dusty *Greene's History of Bay Harbor*, a high school graduation gift from her father, which had been right there on her shelf for years above *Ulysses*. On a Saturday she drops off Emmett and goes to the Historical Society Museum, where she says *microfiche* for the first time. She thinks of fuzzy minnows, darting behind the gray screen with flapping fins.

She reads about the smelting factories and the theater where Christopher Reeve worked. She sees JFK in a boat for the Blessing of the Fleet. She reads about the Lobster Wars, fixed rates for each catch, the lawyers fighting it out, the lobstermen winning. The Rogers and Hammerstein movie filmed downtown in the 50s, lots of locals as extras.

Molly doesn't know what she's looking for, but she takes notes. She wants new lists to mull over and organize.

How sad to have overlooked this information. She'd only had to go as far as the main street. Why hadn't she listened when living people—her grandfather—had told her about it?

She microfiches *Maine artists* and a print by Rockwell Kent comes up. *Sun, Monhegan, Manana.*

She knows just where that is—the view from Burnt Head above the old shipwreck, where Pete had swiped her hat in the cold.

Because she's done the cruise and the Historical Society, because her parents have finally left her alone in her drafty house by the bay, Molly looks around at her possessions. There's nothing very weird. The lumpy, greasy candles, the stones from the beach in bright blue jars. The polka-dotted pillows she'd chosen from TJ Maxx. Aggressively cheery, her sisters had called them.

There are Pete's things, the last batch of paintings in the basement, the same thing over and over—palm trees and beaches—cramming the basement walls.

She could sell them, say her sisters. Take one last look if you want, then dump them all. Her walls should be bare and clean.

With Emmett in bed, she crouches at Pete's bookshelves stacked with monographs, heavy and used, bought by her—slabs of books from sale tables.

At the caviar *Tribune* party there had been big books she remembered: English Gardens, German Castles, Artifacts from China. "Make sure your fingers aren't smudgy," her mother had said. Why would her fingers be smudgy? She'd tried to imagine where big, pretty books would go in her parents' house, how they'd fit on the coffee table between cellophaned hardcovers from the Memorial Library and loose balls of yarn.

Soon after her wedding, Molly decided that prettier books would belong in her own house. Her living room would be weighed down with heavy, bound pages. Emmett would be allowed to touch them.

She'd wrapped up *The Symbolists* for Pete's birthday, clean and shiny, and told him to open it last. "There are too many vowels in a name like Gauguin," said Molly, after they'd had the slices of pound cake Molly made. The cover looked tropical, a little racy with the bare women. He hugged her and kept it out on the table for months, the pages still un-creased.

Pete hadn't corrected her pronunciation or explained why it was spelled that way—that "a" and "u" together sounded much like our plain old "o." The French way seemed more complicated—two letters where one in English would do. These were things Molly found out on her own in the moldy French-English dictionary.

Now *The Symbolists'* pretty cover is torn. But *Writings of a Savage* is un-dusty, with red markings in the margins. The pens Pete liked from the bank.

She reads. And then she begins to laugh like her father, like her Grammy. On the back cover, scrawled like a crazy person, is Pete's last message:

Go to Met. Meet her there.

Met. Like Met Gad Gauguin, the Danish wife, she thought at first. She was fat and she had five children, Molly read. Four of them lived. Someone had written that name over and over in the old dictionary (the girlie handwriting—a girl? Or Pete as a boy?) and it stuck. That's how Molly chose 'Emmett' for her son.

But that was Mette. This is Met. It isn't about the wife.

He means the Met. The Art Club trip in high school. The dirty park with the homeless men and the free food from the Hare Krishnas. Pete fiddling under her skirts on the bus ride home when all she'd wanted to do was sleep.

He had a plan—there it was in red ink. Not off to Monhegan, as she thought, but another island. Because the Twirlie is sure to make it there (She could make it anywhere!) according to the diligent *Tribune.*

How much easier it would be to think of him deserting in a less deliberate way. Drifting away slowly like the houseboat.

The swell inside Molly's chest makes her want to break things. This is not a feeling that is dull.

But neither is it unusual. Her husband left town because the girl he's fucking left too.

The *Copdependent* books her sisters brought say not to do this, not to dwell on the *why*. Dwelling on *why* means she's still trying to fix the problem. Fix her missing husband, find a reason for all the naked girls on beaches in the frames. A better reason than the Twirlie.

Molly looks at the other Gauguin books she bought him, remembers the dusty place in Brunswick, the determined jingle of the door, the man with dandruff behind the counter. He'd placed a plain brown bag around the book as though it was *Playboy*.

"You like this guy, Gauguin?" he said.

"My husband—he's an artist."

"But such a user. And his privates shriveled up."

(Why hadn't she listened then?)

For my Pete, another savage artist, she'd written inside. Not, *I love you.* It had been a bitter Christmas between them, a show put on for Emmett.

She skims the *Savage* book and find more words from her husband in the margins: *Glimmers of having another life. Like being an astronaut. Imagining what that would feel like—seems like an easy option, disappearing. Then the moment passes and it seems impossible again.*

She understands that a shy person can have a steeliness inside and rarely show it. Only when pushed.

It's the same thing that made a shy banker from Paris become an absinthe-addled lover of teenage girls. Living in a hut and wearing a grass skirt. Still, what a depressing one for her husband to link himself to.

Was it just an urge for decadence? Or wanting stories to tell? It's more exciting than the story of staying behind.

Molly wants more letters from Mette the wife. Where are they? Only one in the *Symbolists* book, about selling his favorite Cezanne. In one picture, all the Gauguins are smiling, even Mette, even though her daughter Aline is dead, even though her husband has a serious venereal disease and children from another woman, new Tahitian children to replace the dead daughter. The new mother is just a girl herself, fourteen. Younger by six years than Gauguin's own daughter was when she died.

It feels like bad luck, all this reading. Something sickly could seep out, the yellowed pages rubbing off like a smudge.

So weird to still need each other in this sad, twisted way, she reads in the margins.

She shuts the books.

The new lists come easily in a plain black and white speckled ledger, the kind she'd once used for groceries.

She begins to consider the distance Gauguin traveled, warm in her family home with the fire dying out, Emmett tucked away. At the library, when Mrs. Decker wasn't looking, Molly had positioned her fingers on the globe, Denmark and Polynesia, two opposing hemispheres.

Why? If she figures it out, maybe she'll have something useful to say to Emmett later on. A more definitive reason why he shouldn't take up painting himself.

Plus, Molly knows, letting the true thought surface (Why not?), she wants to know how it happens exactly, the decision to dump the wife as would-be muse.

She writes in her notebook, *Fact: When he stopped touching me, I stopped touching him.*

But after that she has to imagine the Twirlie, even if her sisters' books tell her not to.

It must have been interesting for him to feel the contrast, the sharpness of the Twirlie's limbs, the way he could circle her wrist with his thumb and forefinger. Her ass boney like his, her ribs right there under the skin.

He left the Twirlie in the dark, let himself out of her parents' cottage or wherever it was they went. He sniffed himself for evidence, then found a can by the couch, Miller or Pabst, and dripped what was left on his shirt, his jeans. *Drank too much, had to sleep it off. Didn't have my phone charged.*

Slept where? Molly had said. It seemed like the easiest question.

Pound, he said. *Let myself in the back office.*

You do smell a bit like clams, Molly thought.

The Twirlie thought she was clever because she knew a lot of lyrics, because she got them out in the right order, because she did this with hundreds of songs apparently, night after night in a cruise ship lounge, docked in some hot, sweaty place that required vaccinations. So the *Tribune* said.

There was probably very little mystery left for the Twirlie, which comforted Molly some. All those songs memorized and digested, made meaningless with repetition. She pictured the guitarist propping Karla up, making bad jokes. He wouldn't take himself seriously, not even during the romantic duets. He wanted to be anywhere but there—watching football or drinking in earnest. A pint glass teetered on his amp and he willed it to tip and make sparks so they'd have to cut their shitty set short. No one listened.

Upon her return to Bay Harbor, after her failure as a lounge singer, the Twirlie would begin to have outbursts. This was another way to create adrenalin, now that she wasn't in front of people in shiny dresses every night. She'd have to churn up the mud herself, fight to the point of screaming with her mother. Flirt with someone she shouldn't.

It would be almost the same: heart beating, a flush in her limbs. Release.

Then the guilt. *Wrong, she'd been wrong, she was not a good person.* The Twirlie looked at the tourists in her pretty hometown and thought, *How are all these people happy? How do they do it without drinking?* She didn't wonder about the happiness of the locals because she knew just how miserable they were.

Was it worth it? Molly wondered—the push, the high, the wallow until she needed the adrenalin again? A person like that wasn't apt to live for very long.

After work, Molly microfiches some more and finds the Twirlie's humble beginnings, *Beans of Egypt, Maine* humble, at least on her father's side.

The Twirlie had left town, joined the circus, because she'd had to. And she'd failed at just about everything up until now.

*

Pete's mother Mimi sits on her porch with the chimes and the tall plants, a little forest enclosing her. Grey curls spring from her headscarf. Her silver rings glint. She holds in her lap a worn manila envelope.

"Molliane," she says, rising to hug her. "I'm so glad you came. You look better, much better."

Molly nods. She sits on a torn sun lounger, blue and green stripes.

"I'm so sorry my son is a bit of a turd."

Molly doesn't argue.

"More than a bit. I'd hoped he'd grow out of it but."

There is nothing after the but. Just another opportunity for Molly to disagree. She doesn't. "Thank you," says Molly. Thank you for birthing a turd?

"Here," says Pete's mother, placing the envelope in Molly's hands. "Here are letters. Nine of them. They're meant for Pete but."

"I don't plan on seeing him any time soon."

"No, no. Of course not. I mean, they're meant for Pete, but I'm giving them to you. I want you to have them now."

Molly's weariness feels ingrained. What does she want with old letters? Sent from Pete to his mother, she assumes. How far away had Pete actually gone before now?

"Thank you," Molly says again. Such a benign and useful phrase. "I'm sure Emmett will be glad to have them someday."

"You misunderstand," says Mimi. She looks for her Camels, finds them, sucks in greedily, like her son, showing cheekbones that make her look worldly. "They're not from Peter. They're meant for you and Emmett now. I think you'll find they're worth quite a lot of money."

"Oh," says Molly.

"Do you know this story? The orphanage and the fishmonger from the island?"

"I know about the woman from Monhegan. She cut up fish for a living. She had a daughter."

"And a son. We descend from an orphan, Pete and I. The fish lady dropped a little boy upstate, a century ago. She left a dictionary and these letters. She went back to Monhegan and never left the island again."

Orphan, thinks Molly. *Little girl in a red dress, tap dancing with Daddy Warbucks.* "Why?"

"Who knows why," says Mimi, flicking the stupid question away with her small, quick hands. "She didn't want the baby. She couldn't afford the baby. She wanted to punish the baby's father. She needed to keep the baby a secret. There are so many reasons for letting a child go. No?"

"I've seen the dictionary," says Molly, avoiding the question.

"Yes, I gave this to Peter as a boy. I wanted him to stay interested in his language."

"So maybe you should keep the letters." You could use the money, she means, fingering the tear in the lounger slats.

"They aren't meant for me. They're meant to be passed down. Until now, I think. Now I think they're meant to be sold for quick cash." She smiles. "Gauguin, you see. They are letters from Paul Gauguin. You know him?"

"Not personally," says Molly. "Wait. How is that even possible?"

Mimi laughs. "You'll read the letters. You'll see."

Molly waits. The envelope feels weightless in her lap. Is this a strange joke? Should she laugh? Run away?

But Mimi's isn't laughing. "I always thought you'd lighten him up. I thought he'd be less insane around a strong, funny woman like you. But."

I'm funny? "I couldn't fix him," Molly says. But this matters less. She is seen. Mimi sees her. "Wait, *Gauguin*, Gauguin?"

"Yes. And no, he's not meant to be fixed."

"Paul frigging Gauguin!"

"Yes, a real piece of work, apparently. You'll see. Sell the letters, Molly. Promise me. Don't hang onto them anymore. I think they are very bad luck." A mosquito lands squarely on Mimi's arm, right near the elbow. She slaps it, smearing blood. *Little shit*, she says in French, and Molly understands.

17

PETE HAD ALWAYS SAID museums should be free, all of them, but Molly wants to give something at the Met. *Suggested donation*. She waits for the cashier to make a comment about her ancient student ID.

"Thank you," says the cashier. He tosses the entry clasp on the dirty dollar bills that are her change. His mustache is wispy, dumb-looking.

I haven't been a student—or "Molliane Townsend"—in a very long time. "I'm Mette at the Met," says Molly.

It's on her list of daring things to do, which she composed on the Trailways bus from Bay Harbor. She read this in *Real Simple,* a system for jazzing up a dull or troubled life. Wear the fancy thing to the supermarket or try the foods you thought you hated. So far Molly plans to wear, to Shop N Save, a jean skirt that presses against her stomach in an irritating way. In Manhattan, she'll try pickles again, Gus' garlic kosher dill. To go to the Met is first on this list, followed by "Say out loud, 'I'm Mette at the Met.'"

"As in, Gauguin's wife," Molly tells the mustache. *And there's still time to ask me about my real first name, Molliane.*

"*Meh*-tah. She was Danish," says the cashier. He sucks on something minty. He nods to the next tourist in line.

"I know she was Danish," Molly snaps. She holds her purse close.

She slides a hand along the manila envelope, just to make sure it's still there.

On the wall of the Special Exhibit is a map with pins and the pins have colored heads like BB gun pellets, the kind Molly collected from the lawn after her boy cousins came over to play. Peru, France, Denmark, England, Guadeloupe, Martinique, Tahiti, the Marquesas—all stabbed by little red spheres. She thinks of that postcard in Maine gift shops, the road sign of foreign places, towns that have taken root. Paris, South Paris, China, Poland, Denmark, Peru, Vienna (*Vye*-enna). It's a good measure of how long you've lived in Maine—how amused you are by the postcard.

What if she follows the dead, infected man around? Maybe all his little bobble-headed marks could be her places too. *Research*. It's something writers and artists use to justify almost anything. Off they go. If they make something—a painting, a book—it will all be worth it later on: the hungry kids, the addiction to absinthe. But if they go all that way and make nothing, it will seem like a crazy waste of time.

She has an urge to pluck and rearrange: Maine, Massachusetts, New York. (Someone else is trying to read the map but Molly doesn't budge.) The first time to New York was because of Art Club. Those who'd sold enough crap door to door. Magnet pads with dangling pencils and plastic coin counters and boxes of hardened salt-water taffy, the pastel pieces congealed in wax wrappers and sold for three dollars more than the shop in town. She wondered why there couldn't have been a Townsend "send Molly to NYC" bottle drive or something instead.

But she'd been there, she could say. Just as Gauguin had been to Lima. And here she is again.

Kids skitter around the Post-Impressionist Wing with matching backpacks. They read the placards and take notes, squatting down to lean their paper against the floor. It seems to be a scavenger hunt, a way to prove they've looked at art—Cezanne, Seurat, Van Gogh. She could follow them, tell them facts their teacher has probably left out. *This one, Gauguin, had a penis so sore from fucking girls that it nearly fell off.* A pair of boys hunch near *Two Tahitian Women*, giggling about the boobs.

She feels achy in her back already, a twinge up the lumbar specific to museums and malls. But near the gigglers is something new, a small, unassuming landscape, another one by Gauguin. Somewhere cold, looks like—grassy land buffered by a small, plain island. A cliff that slopes and drops into hard, blue sea.

"Fields By the Sea," says the placard, which could be just about anywhere. *Breton*, it says underneath. Maybe the northern bits of France do look an awful lot like Maine. But what Molly sees is the view of Manana Island from Monhegan. Just like the Rockwell Kent she'd seen, *Sun, Monhegan, Manana.*

(Which gives her an idea. She knows what to do with her husband's art books when she's done.)

She circles the gallery again and purchases *The Lure of the Exotic* for $39.95 in the gift shop. She can write it off, maybe. Research.

In the museum café she orders the cheapest thing, a bottle of Perrier for four dollars, and reads as much from the book as she can. She saves the reprinted letters from Mette for last.

She looks around for more impressionable children with backpacks, then takes out the tiny Swiss Army knife security missed. Incredible. No one notices her would-be weapon in that busy space. Or, if they do, they ignore her—she's not a threat. Another fat woman from away in a famous museum.

She rips a blank page from her notebook and writes her own letter. *Dear Director of the Met.* She requests a meeting. She says she has the goods. She leaves the number of the downtown YMCA.

In Manhattan, everything makes sense, more or less. Molly walks the grid. She looks for tall buildings, north or south. She traces right angles until she finds just what she needs. She's impressed with herself for not getting lost.

At home, she's collected maps for years. In her kitchen there's a drawer filled with folded triple-A routes to places she hasn't been.

To test her, she remembers, Pete had sometimes slipped away in crowded places. The Old Port on New Year's Eve. The Clam Festival in Yarmouth. The B-52's concert at the Civic Center. She'd turn and not see him and try to hold the irritation down but *how could he just go without telling her?* Part of it was not wanting to look foolish, standing there alone, but she also had a genuine concern. How would she find her way back again? She couldn't remember exactly where they'd parked the car. She didn't have enough money in her purse for a bus ticket home.

And then he appeared with ice cream or beer or fried dough, smiling, making it hard to blame him.

On St. Mark's, Molly pauses at the stall with the T-shirts: *Take Me Drunk I'm Home, Emotionally Unavailable* and *Fuck You, You Fucking Fuck.* She'd read in the *Portland Press Herald* that the T-shirt is the modern canvas, which is something she'd also thought, though not in those words. In high school at the new age store she'd noticed the slouchy, frowning boys and pretty summer girls and kept a list behind the cash register: *Dopers Win, Silicon Free, Sleep Is So Last Night.* She wanted to ask about their choices. To endorse all that irony seemed like very bad luck.

But maybe she's over-thinking. It's about whimsy, spontaneity, qualities she doesn't possess in abundance. *Oh I love this, isn't this cute?* Maybe it's about having more expendable cash. How quickly she'd de-tagged new T-shirts from Old Navy before her mother saw.

Her mother doesn't believe that T-shirts can be a window into something—a way to be better. Clothing is meant to last a generation or more.

How good the T-shirts felt before they shrunk in the wash.

I Have Mixed Feelings About New York, she reads on St. Mark's, an alternative to the heart symbol. Exactly what she'd written in the shed when she was sixteen, after seeing the same slogan on the Art Club trip with Pete.

Had she seen it on St. Mark's, the same overpriced shirt in the same window, twenty tears ago?

Then she finds *A Moon and Sixpence* in a bargain bin and a biography by Pola Gauguin, the youngest son, at Strand. She sits on a bench in Tompkins Square Park—the homeless are gone now—and folds fingernail portions of pages to remember.

Where Do We Come From? What Are We? Where Are We Going? The title of the famous painting. They're bar questions, opening lines, Pete had said. *Where are you from? What do you do? Where are you going?* Surely Gauguin had asked women in lodging houses in Brittany and Paris. Obviously Pete had asked these questions at the Thistle.

Her own answers depress her: Bay Harbor. Bank teller. Nowhere. Or, more optimistically: Bay Harbor. Stalker. Maybe Tahiti?

Perhaps she could write it off.

On the subway Molly sits beside a woman so thin she seemed to be decomposing right then and there.

"Excuse me," says Molly, and the woman looks up with eyes that haven't been startled by anything in a very long time. "Where Are We Going?"

"Last stop is City Hall." She slips the ear buds into her turquoise purse and says, "Seaport, right? It's at the end of Fulton—you just keep walking toward the water and you'll see it."

Of course. She's a tourist in Birkenstocks, which no one else wears, even though they're ideal summer walking shoes.

Then she thinks, *cab drivers*. She feels like the Shrimp Princess, her hand a flag she won't put down. On the driver's ID badge is a name Molly hasn't seen before, one with not enough vowels.

"Where *you* going?" he says back to her.

Yes, that comes first. She lets him pull away.

At the hostel she decides not to shower or sleep and stays up all night reading in bed by the light from her phone. Russian, Molly decides, of the black-haired mother and daughter who sleep deeply on the opposite bunk. Their faces are streaky. The mother wakes early, the street still dark. The daughter had one pair of pants, which she puts on sleepily and follows her mother out the door.

She thinks of Emmett, with her parents. Too old for Story Land already.

Gauguin had been a man incapable of being in one place long without fornicating, Molly reads. Wherever he'd been, there were most likely children born. Maybe there are more children than anyone really knows about.

For the last time, she reads the letters, the pages delicate with age. For about ten seconds, she thinks to mail them to the Mette, the long-gone wife, the proper owner—just stamp the right postage and be done.

But where would the pages end up? A dead letter office in Denmark? The moment passes. That would be like throwing them away.

Molly washes her face in the surprisingly clean sink and takes the subway back uptown. The building on 72nd and Broadway has curliecued bits of marble on top—parts Pete would have exact names for, cornices and such. The building has a name like a jazz-age song: the Ansonia.

Karla runs, her fancy purse swinging, dressed for work as though she's going to Shop N Save—baggy khaki pants and a wrinkled shirt, hair in a careless ponytail, all of which Molly can see from the Urban Outfitters across the street. Karla knocks a paperback from a vendor's table and doesn't pause to pick it up. Molly wonders what book it was, and then wonders about the purse, which she'd seen day after day in the window of Slick's on Townsend Avenue. Creamy-looking leather wanting to be sniffed and cradled, big brass buckles that belong on a sailboat. A purse no one in town would feel right about bringing into Ebbtide.

In a flash she pictures them as friends, borrowing accessories.

Then Karla ducks inside, gets swept up into the marble. The sign says AMDA, the American Musical and Dramatic Academy. The doorman nods then glances at Karla's ass as she turns.

In the café next door, which (says the sign) offers discounts for AMDA students and staff, Molly orders an everything bagel with low-fat cream cheese. She walks five blocks up and five blocks down. She goes to Tower Records and tries not to touch the CDs that had been touched by so many others. *Matronly,* she thinks, seeing a reflected slice of herself. She returns to the café and orders a cappuccino, which needs more sugar than she'd expected, the foam disappearing quickly, just an ordinary coffee taste left behind. She looks at *The Lure of the Exotic* again, smudging the cover.

When Karla arrives at 11:57, she notices Molly immediately—a clean jerk of surprise from the neck up. Then she looks away, pretending she hasn't.

Still not great at acting, Molly thinks, and for several seconds she pretends she hasn't seen Karla either. A stapled feeling rises in Molly's throat. She swipes at the onion and garlic crumbs on her dress, little black boogers. *How can this turn out well?*

She stands, banging the saucer with her hip, sloshing the

unfoamed coffee. "Hey," she says. *I've come all this way.* Then louder, "Karla," which forces Karla to feign surprise.

Her forehead is very smooth. Oil of Olay? She keeps a travel bottle in her lovely purse, perhaps.

Then Karla hugs her quickly, hands cold through Molly's top. "Wow!" she says. "What are you doing here?"

Last on the *Real Simple* list, safe in Molly's bag, is, "*Fuck you.* Say it to the Twirlie."

"Sit down," says Molly. "Can you?" Her own voice is tight, small. Not the tone she'd practiced.

"I should eat at my desk. I was late today."

"For a minute? Lord knows when I'll be in Manhattan again." *Warmer, better.*

Karla taps a pack of Camel Lights on her wrist, a gesture Molly has never understood. "Can we stand outside?"

This hadn't been in the blocking. They were to sit down with their widest parts hidden. But outside Karla slouches like Kate Moss, her bag the largest thing about her. She hitches it close to her stomach, and it's hard for Molly not to reach out and touch the hefty strap.

"You came on the theater jitney?" says Karla. "Which show?"

Jitney? Yes—she'd come on the theater bus, which departed from the Y parking lot once a month in summer. The show had been *Phantom*, which Molly had already seen at the Portland Civic Center.

"I'm doing research," Molly says. "At the Met. I'll get the Chinatown bus back." Karla doesn't ask about the research or seem impressed by Molly's willingness to take the Chinatown bus. She shifts the greasy deli bag from one hand to the other, something not very healthy inside, probably. Molly isn't sure what to do with her hands. She considers asking for a drag.

"It's so weird that we ran into each other," says Karla. "The Met's across town."

"Actually, I've been stalking you," says Molly. She smiles. Her own purse strap digs hard into her shoulders. Her skirt flaps as a bus squeals by. "I knew where you worked."

"Gotta love the *Tribune*," says Karla evenly.

Coward, says a golden retriever, sniffing near Molly's bare toes. Into his iPhone the dog walker says, "I know! I met her on J-date." Everyone rushes.

She feels a swell in her gut and blurts, "How's Pete?"

Karla stops smoking and looks at Molly at last. Then she focuses on the butt, on grinding it into a mealy stub with her pointy black boot. It's as squashed as it will ever get and still she twists her ankle back and forth like a dancer, like she's warming herself up for pirouettes.

"Stop doing that," says Molly.

"He's well," she says, choosing a tone devoid of pity or guilt.

"Great," says Molly. This is taking too long—the heaving and unzipping. She should have dug it out earlier, made it accessible.

"This is sick," says Karla. "I have to go."

"Give me a fucking minute," says Molly.

Karla waits, lips pressed. "He's not well. He thinks he's related to Paul Gauguin somehow. 'The bastard son.' He doesn't know how to prove it."

"Great-great grandson, to be exact," says Molly. "But no, there's no way to prove it. Besides the bastard part." She jabs the package into the pretty purse, which is gaping for anyone to steal from. "Here," she says. *And now for the envelope.* Then Molly runs.

"You left him ages ago," the Twirlie calls out, projecting well.

Molly charges toward the 2 train, regally, she hopes. Her Birks slap against the pavement as she feels the hammering of organs inside. *Cancer*, she thinks, *You'll get cancer from smoking too much.* She doesn't know where she put her Metrocard.

On the crowded train someone gets up for her to sit. His hat is tweed.

"When are you due?" the man says.

"Soon," says Molly. "Thank you." She sits, her thighs rubbing up against a teen playing a retro version of Pac Man.

It's so much easier to lie.

"*I sold the last Cezanne*," the collected letters begin, from Mette Gad Gauguin to her husband, printed in *Lure of the Exotic* and neatly sliced by Molly. "*Your children had to eat.*"

Plus two of the unsold vaginas her husband had constructed, cut from the dreadful paintings and sandwiched between pages, ovals of dark purples and greens like algae. *These suck*, Molly had added with a helpful post-it note.

Plus her own pages, ripped from the diary she'd kept in the rock salt tub. The entries about Flip's awesome ass and her own daily urges to flee and how little her husband satisfied her in bed, dated years ago, pages that were chalky at the edges from being pushed so far down the barrel.

It doesn't matter who sees the contents of the package, Molly supposes, Karla or Pete or both. Mette and Molly's words have been delivered.

Just as Gauguin's letters will soon be delivered to the Met. All but one.

In the morning, Molly enjoys the baffled expression on the balding Director's face. *How on earth did a hick from Bay Harbor...* There will be many months of authentication. But eventually there will be a very large check.

She boards the Chinatown bus and sleeps the entire eight hours to Maine.

18

IN HER LOVELY HOUSE ON Townsend Gut, Molly makes book piles, away from Emmett's hands. She packs them in a box that says, *Poland Spring: What It Means to Be From Maine.* She seals it shut with duct tape.

On the ferry the young Captain is new, a grown-up summer boy, but the spiel is the same: the island where the monks had stayed; the island where the fireworks are launched. Molly has tea with half and half. She wears her tourist jacket and no one has to help her with her trolley on the dock. She bypasses the pottery barn, the Fish House, the Lupine Gallery, the artists with easels and hats. She goes to the library (CLOSED says the sign), knocks twice, and unsnaps the bungees. *It's heavy,* she thinks of writing, but they'll figure it out. Instead, with a rich smelling Sharpie, she prints *Take what you want.*

She sees the librarian at her desk though the screen, hunched and glum, staring at a notebook. A husky woman, about her size. "I'm making a donation," Molly calls out. She doesn't wait to hear the thank you.

She hikes to the museum and slides the final Gauguin letter under the locked door of the entrance. (Isn't anyone open today?) One letter should stay there, on Monhegan.

She has a large cone with sprinkles and then takes a picture of the hermit shack on Manana. When the return ferry comes, she sits on the top deck and leans over the side to see. “Careful,” says someone from away. “I won’t be jumping in.”

“I won’t be either,” she says, and the tourist laughs.

She takes the last book from her backpack, the French-English dictionary. She waits for the tourists to look the other way. She traces the letters all the way down the page, *MetteMetteMetteMetteMette.* Then she drops it, watching the weight splash and sink, the cover flapping open just below the surface like a dead thing trying to float. But it doesn’t float. It sinks to the bottom and it’s done.

There is Emmett, to be picked up soon, wanting cocoa at Ebbtide. There is Flip, ready to sneak them double portions.

There is the sea around her—constant, steely. It isn’t teal or midnight or any of the complicated shades. It’s blue. She can paint it if she wants.

Epilogue:

Emmett

IT'S CLEAR FROM THE beginning that Emmett won't be a painter. Still, at fourteen he visits his father in Manhattan, where they go skating in Central Park. Or, where his father pays for Emmett and Karla to skate as he smokes cigarettes from the edge of the rink. Pete looks skinny and chapped, standing there alone in sneakers. Between cigarettes, his knuckles needle the pockets of his old windbreaker. *You're from Maine, for Chrissake,* thinks Emmett, trying to keep up with Karla as a Go Go's song blares. Doesn't the man own gloves?

Karla wears a skating outfit: earmuffs, black tights and a skirt that barely covers her ass. She can skate backward and do figure eights, and she smells like a citrusy cake. She looks beautifully sad, like she's been working on it a while. She calls his father Frenchie, a name he'd hated in school. She pays the bulk of the rent.

Emmett sleeps on their frosted white couch and worries about making smudges. Everything is white except his father's paintings, crammed on all the walls. Brown women on beaches and a saronged man standing just like Jesus. The apartment is blocks away from the Met, where Pete can sketch the Symbolists whenever he wants.

It makes no sense to Emmett, the practice of copying the Masters, over and over. It makes no sense for his father to read and re-read Gauguin's letters from Maine, framed and mounted in the Post-Impressionist wing, which the Met had acquired some years back. An anonymous donor.

The letters prove nothing, Emmett knows.

When his father goes to the museum, Emmett stays in the apartment to snoop. He reads Karla's old issues of *Backstage Magazine*, the cruise auditions circled in lime-green ink.

Then Emmett takes the Chinatown bus back to New England and won't see his father again until high school graduation.

At Bay Harbor High, the art teacher invites Emmett to make sea assemblages after school. His mother doesn't like this idea, which is part of the appeal. It's dark down there in the basement, and the old teacher doesn't wear a bra. For a full spring Emmett tolerates the drippy glue gun and the sprawl of dead sea urchins. The teacher's waist-high nipples blare through. Emmett can't think of what to say to the pale, too-quiet girls around the table.

Then, in the rock salt tub, he finds his mother's journals with pages ripped out and, in between, her determined notes from the Bay Harbor Library: her microfiche research, the family tree she'd sketched, Paul Gauguin at the very top. There's a postcard from the Met of a painting called "Fields By the Sea," and *Monhegan!* in his mother's neat, triumphant hand.

In red ink Emmett circles one word on the postcard, right after the Gauguin title. The word is "Breton," which Emmett knows to be in France, not Maine. It isn't hard to find on Wikipedia that Paul Gauguin actually died in the Marquesas—a gravestone to prove it. Complications from a sex disease, his dick covered in sores like the mosquito bites Emmett scratches and scratches on his legs and arms until they bleed. There's a black and white photograph of the *tiki* gravestone, carved by Gauguin himself. *Savage*, it says, marking the burial spot 5,631 miles away from Maine.

Something fastens in Emmett's brain as he sees the photo of the dead artist's grave online. *Relief.* It's all made up, this family lore of being related to greatness. Just another puzzle for his mother to consider, once Pete the Painter left.

Emmett quits Art Club. Then he switches from French to Spanish.

"*Pourquoi?*" says the hunched man who taught them. "You are the son of a French speaker. It is in your blood."

So is adultery, Emmett thinks, but he doesn't know how to say it in French.

"It's not pretty," he says instead, then ducks away to his locker. His parents, he means, their messes and patterns. They're fuck-ups—they can't help it. He doesn't know many parents who aren't.

Emmett buries the journals back in the tub. He helps his mother dry the dishes. He thanks her for dinner and she smiles at him, reaching to put her tea mug away, humming the same terrible 80s songs. He wants to run from her and cling to her at the same time.

Emmett will uncover truths. He'll argue about which facts to follow and get paid to do this. He'll be pre-law. His mother's face will burst open when she announces this to strangers, the first Townsend to go for a full four years, and out of state. At Target she'll hover and want to buy matching yellow bean bags, one for his roommate too. Emmett will talk her out of this. She'll insist on new socks and underwear, at least, and a laundry bag with the Maine state coat of arms: *Dirigo: I Lead*. He'll use his own money (*Why?* his mother will say), saved from working summers at the pound, to pay for a simple lamp, a sturdy stapler, his books with rigid spines. His mother will write tuition checks without complaint and he won't question this, where all the money has come from. Certainly not from his father.

He'll see his father at weddings and funerals and his mother during holidays and he'll marry a pre-med woman of Irish decent. They'll enroll their children in sports programs and hang only photographs in their home. They'll hope to God their daughters won't discover the vaginas their grandfather painted long ago, some of which can be seen on the faded walls of Bay Harbor businesses. *Flowers*, Emmett is prepared to answer. Then he'll hold his daughters tight and change the subject.

It could be true, he thinks sometimes, once his daughters are too old to clasp. It could be. But where is the evidence?

The bottom of the sea, his mother answers sometimes, long after she's gone, in a dream he can't dispel. Her pleased expression. Grey wisps from a loose bun.

Le fond de la mer, he remembers, waking. A language he hasn't spoken in years.

Acknowledgments

Thank you:

To my agent, Stacia Decker, for believing in *Off Island*.

To Cynthia Brackett-Vincent and Eddie Vincent of Encircle Publications for saying yes. To designer Deirdre Wait for the blue boat and bright sky. To Mary Bisbee-Beek for fearless publicity.

To Jeremy Gavron, Peter Turchi, Antonya Nelson, Joan Silber, Jim Shepard, Judith Grossman, and CJ Hribal, my brilliant teachers/mentors in the MFA Program for Writers at Warren Wilson College.

To early (and late) readers Jill Kaplan Tupper and Lisa Mandeville, who share an appetite for fiction and a knack for clear critiques.

To the Mullen House Education Center in Becket, MA, The Writers Room in NYC, New Jersey Transit (Northeast Corridor Line), Central Park (various benches), and Kripalu Center for Yoga and Health in Stockbridge, MA (various meditation cushions), for valuable time and space.

To Joni Mitchell, James Taylor, Prince, Brandi Carlile, and the stellar musicians of the Berkshires for necessary distractions.

To photographer Elaina Mortali for capturing a moment of joy.

To the Metropolitan Museum of Art, where I first stumbled upon Paul Gauguin's letters from Polynesia to his wife, Mette

Gad, in the summer of 2002. That exhibit, Lure of the Exotic, highlighted Gauguin's appropriation of Polynesian custom. It also allowed me to imagine, through his messy relationship with Mette, his desire for connection. It showed me, too, just how fond he was of fornication.

To the residents of Monhegan Island, Maine, for tolerating this summer person. Special thanks to the Monhegan Museum, where the hermit based on Ray Phillips came to life, and to the Balmy Days II, which got me there from here. Thanks to Lisa Brackett for planting seeds and making donuts.

To my father, Stanley Roger Tupper Sr. (1921-2006), for making me a Mainer.

To Bobby Sweet, who knows what it takes to maintain a writing life and lives with me anyway. Thank you for making me laugh, daily, in spite of myself.

To Mette Gad Gauguin, who sacrificed for "pure color." I hope I got the portrait right.

Sources

Barnes, Rachel, ed. *Artists by Themselves: Gauguin*. London: Bracken Books, 1990.

Bashkoff, Tracey. *A Century of Painting: From Renoir to Rothko*. New York: The Solomon R. Guggenheim Foundation, 2003.

Bolton, Linda. *Gauguin: The History and Techniques of the Great Masters*. 1987. Reprint. Edison: Chartwell Books, 1997.

Danly, Susan. S*ide by Side on Monhegan: The Henri Circle and the American Impressionists*, Monhegan, ME: Monhegan Museum, 2004.

Deci, Edward L. *Life on a Remote Fishing Island, 1920-1950*. Monhegan: Monhegan Museum, 2007.

Fuller, Ruth Grant. *Monhegan: Her Houses and Her People, 1780-2000*. Melrose, MA: Mainstay Publications, 2001.

Gauguin, Paul. *The Writings of a Savage*, edited by Daniel Guérin. New York: The Viking Press, 1974.

Gauguin, Pola. *My Father, Paul Gauguin*, translated by Arthur G. Chater. 1937. Reprint. New York: Hacker Art Books, 1988.

Hale, John R. "The Fearsome Sea." *Age of Exploration*. 1966. Reprint. New York: Time Incorporated, 1971. 21-28.

The Hermit of Manana. Elisabeth B. Harris, Producer/Director. Eye Heart Films, 2006.

Hollman, Eckhard. *Paul Gauguin: Images from the South Seas*. 1996. Reprint. New York: Prestel Pegasus Library, 2001.

Howard, Michael, and The Musée Gauguin, Tahiti. *Eyewitness Art: Gauguin*. New York: Dorling Kindersley, 1992

Ives, Colta, and Susan Alyson Stein. *The Lure of the Exotic: Gauguin in New York Collections, The Metropolitan Museum of Art, New York*. New Haven: Yale University Press, 2002.

Kay, Rob. *Hidden Tahiti and French Polynesia*. Berkeley: Ulysses Press, 2005.

Kjellgren, Eric, and Carol S. Ivory. *Adorning the World: Art of the Marquesas Islands, The Metropolitan Museum of Art, New York*. New Haven: Yale University Press, 2005.

Le Bot, Marc. *Gauguin's Noa Noa*, translated by Shaun Whiteside. 1996. Reprint. New York: Assouline Publishing, 2003.

Mathews, Nancy Mowll. *Paul Gauguin: An Erotic Life*. New Haven: Yale University Press, 2001.

Melville, Herman. *Typee*. 1846. Reprint. New York: Quality Paperback Book Club, 1996.

Oleksy, Walter. *Mapping the Seas*. New York: Scholastic Inc., 2002

Sion, Georgia. *Gauguin's South Seas*. New York: Universe, 1992.

Notes

Part One:
The Painter

1) p. 37: "*I have always wanted a mistress who was fat, and I have never found one. To make a fool of me, they are always pregnant...*"
Paul Gauguin's words, as quoted in *Lure of the Exotic.* I first read Paul's letters to Mette at The Met, where I took frantic notes. (*Wait. He's writing to his wife about his mistress?*) I later tracked them down in this exhibit publication.

2) p. 51: "Lizzie knew there was a place called St. Cloud's upstate."
A nod to John Irving. St. Cloud's is the fictional orphanage in *The Cider House Rules.*

Part Two
Pete

3) p. 58: "As a boy Pete had spells sometimes, just like that girl in the Ben Folds song—*She had spells where she lost time.*"
From "Zak and Sara" by Ben Folds (*Rockin' the Suburbs*, 2001).

4*)* p. 59: "(Later, Pete's own son would like the whale part in *Finding Nemo*, the waves gathering inside the mammoth, fishy ribs.)"
Please watch this scene on YouTube.

5) p. 64: "He wrote, in a tiny pink card, *Really like your peaches, wanna shake your tree.*"
From my high school anthem, "The Joker," by Steve Miller Band (*The Joker*, 1973). Credited songwriters are Steve Miller, Eddie Curtis, and Ahmet Ertegun. (I wonder if they debated about which fruit to use.)

4) p. 64: "He read a little from a novel she'd left open, a story about an Old West woman living in a place called Mineral Palace. He caught the phrase 'finite use' and something budged inside as he read on. It was about having a finite use for someone, using a person between periods of badness or confusion or loneliness."
A reference to Heidi Julavits' novel, *The Mineral Palace.*

5) p. 70: "His mother gave him the *Griffin and Sabine* books, which were not at all girlie."
As a young adult I loved this series by Nick Bantock, which began with *Griffin and Sabine: An Extraordinary Correspondence.* (I could slip actual letters out of glued-in envelopes.) They're called epistolary novels; I think of them as picture books, modern adaptations of Gauguin's *Noa Noa.*

6) p. 117: "And little Emmett will hear stories about his father the Famous Painter, who lived out his last days as a savage, *able to work, love and die.*"
I paraphrase Paul Gauguin here, as quoted in *Lure of the Exotic.*

Part Three
The Wife

7) 145: "The first mention of Tahiti came in October: *May the day come (soon perhaps) when I'll flee to the woods on an island in Oceania, there to live in ecstasy, calm, and art. With a new family by my side, far from this European scramble for money. There, in Tahiti, in the silence of the beautiful tropical nights, I'll be able to listen to the soft murmuring of my heart in harmony with the mysterious beings around me. Free at last, without financial worries and able to love, sing and die.*"
From *Writings of a Savage.*

8) 147: "From Papeete he'd written, *Farewell, dear Mette, dear children. Love me, and when I'm back we will get married again. Which means, today I'm sending an engagement kiss to you.*"
From *Paul Gauguin: Images of the South Seas.*

9) 150: "He wrote, *My studio is very handsome and I can assure you time goes by quickly... What a pity you have not tasted this Tahitian life; you would never want to live any other way.*"
From *Writings of a Savage.*

10) "When he was sick he wrote more often: *I'm spitting blood—a small bucket's worth...and my hospital treatment is twelve francs per day.*"
From *Paul Gauguin: Images of the South Seas.*

11) "She skimmed, until—
I'm soon to be the father of a half-caste; my charming Dulcinea has decided to lay an egg."
From *Writings of a Savage.* (You can't make this stuff up.)

Part Three
Molly

12) p. 163: "Once, bored and nervous at the dentist's, she read a *New Yorker* story, the Vogue and People taken. It was a story about having "a suitable insanity." All men had one, apparently, such as "devotion to a ball team" or a favorite beer. But for the writer (or the person the writer pretended to be in the story—Molly realized there might be a difference, though she doubted it), beer or sports weren't insane enough. To be suitable, the insanity had to be a deeper. It had to be something that took a very long time to understand."
See Alice Munro's short story, "Vandals."

13) p. 199: "As that Canadian, Margaret Atwood, wrote, in another book Molly kept in the guest room, inside the imperfect husband is a perfect husband maybe, just waiting to be lured out by Molly for good."
See Margaret Atwood's short story, "Happy Endings."

About the Author

LARA TUPPER'S DEBUT NOVEL, *A Thousand and One Nights* (Harcourt/Untreed Reads), is an autobiographical tale about breaking the trajectory of career, marriage, family. Her linked short story collection, *Amphibians*, is forthcoming from Leapfrog Press in 2020 (winner, Leapfrog Fiction Prize). Her short fiction was runner up for the 2019 Nicholas Schaffner Award for Music in Literature; her prose has appeared in *The Believer, Nowhere Magazine, Dogwood Journal, Epiphany* and other literary publications. Born in Boothbay, Maine, Lara now writes, teaches and performs in Western Massachusetts. A jazz/pop vocalist, her latest album is This Dance. laratupper.com

CPSIA information can be obtained
at www.ICGtesting.com
Printed in the USA
FSHW010357190919
62155FS